Rescuing Liberty

Perseverance Book 1

Amanda Washington
www.amandawashington.net

For my momma:
You never once told me it was impossible to fly.
Instead you showed me how to trust God and jump.
Thank you.

Acknowledgements

First and foremost I thank God—for just being, blessing, and forgiving.

Special thanks to my sister, Apryl Risoldi, who encouraged me to put my dreams on paper.

Without the love and encouragement of my husband, Meltarrus, and our five sons I would have quit long ago. I love you guys! Thank you for being there for me.

To my editors—Krista Darrach and George Hill who poured over the story many times, and were never afraid to point out my numerous mistakes—thank you. I couldn't have done it without you both!

I have been blessed with incredibly supportive sisters, cousins, aunts, uncles, parents, grandparents, and in-laws. I want you all to know how truly invaluable your love, prayers, and support have been.

Sincere thanks to the many people who encouraged me, including but not limited to the following: David Antonio, Pam Armstrong, Kenton Brine, Pam Busch, Terry Busch, Cindy Call, Trina Cardoza, Michele Cardwell, Deena Cornish, Kim Corona, Jim Darrach, Chris Fletcher, Melanie Fletcher, Doug Fromm, Faith Hahn, Jason Harnack, Nichole Krieger, Robert Krieger, Trina Krieger, Aaron Lamb, Kim Legato, Molly McGraw, Hoyt (Byron) McNair, Wayne Perryman, Noelle Pierce, Rob Pomeroy, JD Revene, Kelli Rodriguez, Pete Scholl, Cathy Sitzes, Clark Sitzes, Sue Smith, Lisa Tucker, Chris Washington, Vickie Westfall, Elizabeth Whitworth, Gary Wolcott, Nesha Wright, all my Facebook friends, and anyone else I may have missed. Your belief in me kept me typing and editing, even when I didn't want to. Thank you all!

1: Wasteland

Liberty

"America will never be destroyed from the outside. If we falter and lose our freedoms, it will be because we destroyed ourselves." —Abraham Lincoln

***June 7

With a dagger in one hand and my best friend—a Smith and Wesson Sigma—in the other, I analyzed shadows outside the window. My red curls were haphazardly pulled through the back of a navy-blue Mariners baseball cap. I gripped the gun and glanced at the letters I'd carved dangerously close to the artery on my left wrist: WWL.

Crazy much, Libby?

"Nice warm jacket, soft-padded cell, three square meals a day. Doesn't sound so bad, does it?" I asked the stuffed bear lying near my feet.

Frog—as my niece Megan lovingly named the bear—didn't look impressed by my wit. Frog had been well loved, and it showed. He was missing an eye, and the hole on his arm was visible around the edges of a Band-Aid. He stared at me, looking terrified of being left behind.

"That's not fair." I nudged Frog with my toe in an effort to redirect his gaze.

He rolled completely over, and his big brown eye continued to play on my conscience. I sighed.

"How do you feel about Canada?"

Tucking the gun into the back of my jeans, I reached down and picked up the bear.

"Don't worry, Frog. Canada will be better. Promise."

Hope.

I shoved Frog into my large hiking backpack next to a crumpled family portrait, a few bottles of water, two lighters, a small journal, a couple pens, a roll of duct tape, my sleeping bag, and a wind-up flashlight radio. The flashlight radio was turned on to scan for stations daily, but so far had only found static.

Stretching, I scrunched up my nose at the odor assaulting me from my arm pits. It had been days since I'd last bathed in a stream outside Olympia, and I felt as disgusting as I smelled.

My stomach growled, reminding me of matters more essential than my neglected hygiene. I eagerly reached into the front pocket of my filthy jeans, when I remembered that the peanuts I was seeking had been breakfast.

A person could starve to death in this city.

Tens of thousands already had.

My temporary shelter reeked of death and human waste. Littering the floor, children's toys and books looked lonely and neglected under a thin layer of dust. The outlines of various footprints told stories of survivors desperately searching for something—anything.

This had once been my sister Anna's spotlessly clean home; now it was ransacked and damaged beyond recognition. Just the sight of the cupboard doors hanging from their hinges would no doubt send the obsessive-compulsive Anna into hysterics.

She couldn't see the cupboards anymore.

Anna had tormented and terrorized me throughout our childhood, but she hadn't proven tough enough when it really counted.

Each breath is a gift.

The last time I'd been in this house was for Thanksgiving. Only seven months ago I sat at the bar and obligingly chopped whatever Anna threw my direction for the holiday dishes. Her husband, Tom, was on his hands and knees pretending to be a horse for their two-year-old twins, Megan and Martin. He bucked and reared as they giggled and hooted. If I closed my eyes I could still hear their laughter.

Their bodies remained where I found them, huddled together peacefully in Anna and Tom's bed. No stab or bullet wounds. No blood.

No hope.

This had been their first house, and Anna had turned it into a comfortable home. Family pictures littered the wall beside me—some hanging askew, others broken and lying randomly on the floor. Obscenities were carved into the coated face of their fifty-six inch flat screen TV. Deep slashes ran across once overstuffed couches, and the filling covered the floor like mounds of snow.

Lives spent collecting these material possessions—all this crap—and none of it mattered. Nothing here had saved my sister's family from their fate.

Another useless tear slid down my dirty cheek.

My sister's family was dead, and this house was their tomb. I ground my teeth as the desire to kill those who'd desecrated it overwhelmed me.

No. Judgment is not mine to pass.

I fought for control over my emotions, put down the imaginary gavel, and considered the evening view outside the window. The sun was setting on the remains of the once-prosperous city of Olympia, Washington. Calming lines of reds and oranges ran across the sky, contrasting with the dark, sinister shadows on the ground.

Early June displayed an impressive amount of greenery and flowers. Roses—unaffected by the destruction—bloomed in every color alongside ruined buildings. Lush bushes and healthy grass grew obliviously around scattered human remains.

Nature donned a convincing façade as it attempted to hide the passing of humankind. Intoxicating fragrances of lilacs and hyacinths put forth a valiant effort, but couldn't mask the reek of decay.

I rubbed my tired eyes, slipped my backpack over my aching shoulders, and headed for the back door. My fingers instinctively massaged the scar on my wrist while I scrutinized the shadows of the backyard, watching for movement. I opened the door, took another deep, steadying breath, and stepped into the dusk.

Looking back at the house, I noticed that Tom never did get around to fixing the screen the twins destroyed. A simple chore left undone, yet it was too much.

My throat constricted.

Breathe.

I stuffed the memories back behind the locked door in my mind. I'd open it someday when I was ready to welcome the madness. Even now I could hear the nightmares knocking, taunting me with a way to ease the pain, a way to forget.

Not today—maybe tomorrow.

Bowing my head, I crossed myself. No organized "religion" had ever felt right—but this Catholic gesture comforted me somehow. In one simple hand signal to God I confirmed my continued belief and petitioned for His aid.

As I headed out, the gun pressed into the small of my back. The discomfort served as a constant reminder of the blood on my hands. "Thou shalt not murder," the commandment declared, and as a child, I'd been taught the biblical difference between "kill" and "murder," but what of self-defense? Is it more of a slap-on-the-hand than a burn-for-eternity sentence?

Perhaps the Almighty would allow an attorney?

Of course all the good attorneys would be in hell ...

It's hard to stay clean while swimming in murky water. When it came down to kill or die, my lineage as a child of Cain had been proven. But every day I prayed for redemption while checking both 16-round magazines of the 9mm; prayed I wouldn't have to use them.

How did the line between right and wrong get so blurry?

I walked until the sun breached the horizon, hopped over a fence, and slid into a small portable shed. Lawn care equipment and a tricycle frame were the sole contents;

nothing of use. Disappointed, I peeked outside to check out the area, and was surprised to find an apple tree. Licking my lips in anticipation, I watched, waited, and listened. My mouth watered from the thought of digging my teeth into a crisp, Washington, Gala apple.

Nothing about my surroundings was threatening; just a small backyard behind a two-story home. A chain-linked fence bordered knee-high grass. There were no abnormal movements or sounds.

Hunger burned within me, melting my paranoia and liquefying my patience.

Apple pie, apple turnover, apple crisp, apple dumplings ... torture!

With my gun still at my back, I could stick the dagger in my teeth and scale the tree like Rambo. I'd climbed trees as a child.

How hard could it be?

Footsteps came from my right. I dropped into a crouch and prayed intensely for invisibility.

Please, God, don't let anyone find me.

A boy who looked about thirteen, rough and tough, with scrawny arms, long legs, and the awkward stance of a pre-teen, hopped the fence and sneaked up to the tree. He looked around nervously and embarked on his climbing mission, lurching and sliding as he struggled to find his footing on the trunk.

The hem of his jeans caught on a small twig and as he kicked to free his leg he fell to the ground with a loud thump. Instinct kicked in, and I shuffled my feet, preparing to run out and help him.

'No!'

The voice of the *call* fell on my heart, commanding me to remain hidden. More powerful than words, the *call* flooded my senses with understanding, cautioning me against revealing myself to the child.

No? He's just a boy. He needs me!

Another rugged figure came skulking from the boy's hiding place: a man with deep-set eyes, dark hair, and a lean, muscular build. He moved fluidly, like a hunter. Not a hunter of animals, though. "Hunter" was what I called those who had escaped the burden of their conscience. They lurked in the shadows and preyed on the defenseless.

I winced as the child smiled and encouraged the man's approach.

Look what You did!

I glanced at the shed's ceiling, adjusting my cap as I argued with the *call*.

Just a kid and now he's in the hands of some hunter. What are You doing?

I felt no response as the hunter crept over, braced the boy's foot, and boosted him up within reach of the first branch. The branch creaked under the youth's build.

I watched hopelessly as the boy stretched, bent, reached, and finally made contact with the first apple. He plucked it and stashed it in a pocket.

Good boy! Fill your own pockets first.

The child collected several more apples, storing the first few in his pockets and then begrudgingly tossing the remainder down to his companion. The hunter helped the boy down, and looked around nervously while the child bent and emptied the apples he'd collected into his pack. When the kid stood up, the large butcher knife he wielded glinted in the sun.

"Let's go." The man twisted back around as the boy plunged the knife into his stomach.

2: Changes

Connor

***Fifteen weeks earlier - February 24*

A guard pushed open the heavy, oak door. Late February sunshine poured into the old courthouse, banishing the shadows of winter. I walked out onto the steps followed closely by my client, Fredrick Adams. The media descended upon us; cameras flashed, microphones waved, and phony smiles lit up the faces of the press.

An unfamiliar woman muscled her way to the front of the crowd, and pointed an NBS labeled microphone at my client. "Mr. Adams, are you pleased with the court's verdict?"

She was trendy and tasteful in her tight, pinstriped business skirt and matching jacket. The silky, white shell underneath was cut low enough to display a decent amount of cleavage from my elevated vantage point. Her short, blonde hair accentuated a tanned, firm neck, glowing under a single strand of pearls.

"Of course." I smiled and looked into her blue eyes.

The microphone wielder turned her attention on me. "Mr. Dunstan, as the counsel representing Mr. Adams, what can you tell viewers about allegations of your client's involvement with the illegal sale of plans for the new 877 jet to Accelerated Aerotech?"

"Just another greedy employer's feeble attempt to conceal wrongful termination. My client was the victim of age discrimination, and today his employer has been schooled on the consequences for such actions." I paused for affect, and looked into the camera.

A black limo pulled up to the curb below us. The chauffeur climbed out of the driver's seat, walked around the car, and opened the back door facing me. I nodded when I caught his eye.

"If there had been any evidence to support such an outlandish speculation, my client would not be the victor today." I smiled and posed once more as cameras clicked and other reporters fought for my attention.

Lowering my voice so only the woman in front of me could hear, I whispered, "I'd love to discuss this matter further, but I have a client waiting." I reached for her unoccupied left hand and squeezed her fingertips. Her cheeks reddened at my wink, and when I pulled my hand back, my business card remained in her grasp. She glanced at the card and her eyes widened. Perfectly glossed lips spread into a dimpling smile as she slid my contact information into her jacket pocket.

Client in tow, I waded through the throng of reporters pointing microphones and cameras in our direction, and climbed into the back seat next to my business partner, Justin Brayer. The chauffeur closed the door behind us, regained his own seat, and the car pulled slowly away from the mass of cameras and leering reporters that always followed high profile cases.

The chauffeur knocked on the privacy glass that separated us.

"Yes." Justin answered.

"Excuse me Sir, but did Mr. Adams park in this lot or the next?"

Frederick motioned to the lot in front of us. "You can just drop me off here." He turned to face me. "Thank you, Connor. For everything."

I smiled at another satisfied client. "My pleasure." I extended my hand. "I'll give you a ring when they send the paperwork over."

Frederick shook my hand as the limo came to a stop.

The chauffeur opened the door and waited.

"And remember," I said to Frederick's retreating back. "If anyone tries to contact you about what happened today—or these bogus allegations—send them my way."

"Will do." He gave a stiff nod. "Thanks again."

Once we were alone, Justin motioned toward the crowded courthouse steps out the back window. "Quite the crowd today."

I glanced behind us. "Vultures."

He chuckled. "Now that's not nice, Connor. They're only performers, acting under the directions of their employers." He grabbed the bottle of wine he'd been chilling, and tilted it toward me in question.

It wasn't quite noon yet, and Justin had already popped the cork of a Château d'Yquem. I smiled and nodded.

Associate, not friend.

In no way was I delusional enough to think of Justin as a friend. I kept my proverbial dagger aimed at his back, awaiting any sign that his destruction would be more beneficial than our partnership. I knew his love for me was equally self-gratifying. It's what made the game so fun.

He poured and handed me a glass. "The new blonde from NBS ... would you consider her a vulture as well? It didn't look like you'd mind her taking a bite out of your flesh."

I shrugged. "What's the point in being successful if I can't savor the victory dance?"

He laughed and shook his head as I fantasized about the blonde. She'd call. They always did.

"To another win?" I held up my wineglass for a toast.

"No." He raised his glass and lightly tapped mine. "To the purchase of fifty shares of Accelerated Aerotech stock."

***June 8

Wow. Sixty-two day silent treatment. That's gotta qualify her for some sort of record.

I stared down at my brother's twelve year old daughter, Ashley, as she rested on her air mattress, facing the wall. I let out a breath. "I won't be gone long."

Ashley ignored me, just like she had for the past two months.

Our shelter was the large walk-in safe inside my brother's store. Originally he and his wife had been with us, but now it was just Ashley and I. Pleasantly loud when they were here, the loss of Jacob and Cathy had turned the safe into a quietly hostile environment.

I grabbed my Glock and switchblade from the top of a nearby shelving unit. The blade went into the front pocket of my jeans, and I slid the gun into a pouch inside my jacket. Stepping up to the door, I spun the dial through the correct series of numbers and opened it. I walked into my brother's computer parts store and locked the safe behind me.

Jacob loved this place. He'd always been a geek, fascinated with taking apart and rebuilding computers. I closed my eyes and remembered how wide he'd smiled the day he signed the papers to make this store his own. He had stood behind the counter, jingling the keys at me, grinning like a jackal.

I looked around his new purchase, apprehensively noticing the fading paint and unorganized shelves. My eyes must have reflected my thoughts, because Jacob countered my skepticism.

"I know it needs some work." He tapped on the cracked countertop in front of him. "But it's *my* store. *My* dream."

"If it makes you happy." I shrugged and smiled.

"More happiness than *you* can imagine." He picked up the rag before him and polished the cash register.

"What's that supposed to mean? I'm happy." I walked forward until I was across the counter from him. "I'm on a streak. Just won my tenth case. And this morning I stumbled upon a tidbit that's sure to discredit the witness in the McPhearson trial."

He narrowed his eyes. "You'll never be truly happy until you stop trying to be someone else."

I chuckled and held out my hands. "Hey bro, what you see is what you get."

"You're not foolin' me. I know what lies beneath that overly-ambitious, womanizing shell."

"Oh really?" I leaned against the counter and showed Jacob my teeth. "Enlighten me."

He stared at me, unaffected by my counterfeit smile. "Nope. That's cheating. You cannot be rebuilt, until you are destroyed."

I backed up and bowed deeply. "As always, Master Yoda, you are both wise and cryptic."

You cannot be rebuilt, until you are destroyed.

I let out a deep breath as I looked around Jacob's thrashed store. Glass from the busted windows crunched beneath my shoes. Multiple shelves were tipped over; spilling merchandise upon the floor, and spray painted walls reflected the anger of the vandals.

Destroyed, like Jacob's dream?

Well how you gonna rebuild it now, Bro?

I skulked out of the building, and into the crisp early morning. I intended to go north, but somehow ended up to the east, in front of what remained of my brother's home. It was careless and foolish to allow myself to fall into a pattern, but somehow this was always the first place I came to when I left the safe.

I bent down and picked up a handful of ashes. The wind filtered through my fingers, blowing the dust away. I'd started the fire that burned this place down; a funeral pyre for my brother. There hadn't been time to bury him and Cathy, and burning was the only thing I'd been able to think of at the time.

I turned to leave and saw the flicker of a curtain in a neighboring house.

This is too dangerous, Jacob. I can't come back.

I took one last look at the building remains. I'd done a thorough job, and there wasn't much left to see. Grey ash, knee deep in areas with occasional metal remains that hadn't been completely destroyed. Something shiny caught my eye, so I waded through the cinders toward it.

The two inch tall, bronze colored man held a trophy that declared, *'World's greatest dad'*. I turned it over and read the inscription: *'I love you Daddy, love Ashley'*. I brushed the treasure off and pocketed it.

The sun was starting to come up, so I walked a few blocks over to Jacob's secretary's house. She'd been out of town when the riots hit, and we'd already raided her place for food, but what I needed should still be there. I entered cautiously—my gun drawn—and crept up the stairs into the master bathroom. I started searching through drawers: lotion, perfume, powder.

Why do women need so much junk?

Hairspray, gel, mousse: a whole drawer full of nothing but hair products. I opened the cabinet under the sink.

Bingo.

A box and bag were in the cabinet before me.

Oh crap! Two kinds.

I picked up the box and looked inside. A small instruction guide rested atop the contents, complete with visual aids.

Inside her?

The image of me trying to explain to Ashley how to insert the things popped into my head. I hastily put the box back and grabbed the bag.

I'm not ready for this.

Then I dropped it, startled by the scream that pierced the air.

3: Redemption

Liberty

No, no, no!

The nauseating sound made the sight impossible to deny, as the boy pulled the knife from the hunter's flesh. The dying man's mouth formed an "O" as his hands moved over the wound. "You. You ba—" he started, and then swaggered back and forth a few times before finally toppling over.

The grass turned red around him. The cool morning air became steam where it brushed against the warm blood. My mind made a feeble attempt to detach itself from my senses.

So it wasn't Professor Plum in the dining room with the candle stick. It was the skinny kid in the apple orchard with the knife.

The game of *Clue* popped into my thoughts, redirecting my focus to a reality where murder was only a game. Blinking, I tried to picture the layout of the *Clue* board as I fought to maintain control of my queasy stomach.

Must remain quiet.

Blood dripped from the knife the boy held. I focused on breathing as he methodically extracted the apples, and other items of interest, from the man's pockets.

The kitchen was in one corner, but what was on the other side of the ballroom?

Attempts to escape were unsuccessful. I couldn't look away as the child—who should have been enjoying his summer vacation—wiped the blood from his knife on the fallen man's shirt.

Not fallen ... murdered. By a child!

He was so callous, calm, and calculating. His big, sweet, trustworthy eyes did not flicker. His breathing did not quicken, his hands did not shake. He had been prepared.

Premeditated.

He was perfectly at ease taking a life—a child hunter. My head found its way between my knees.

Passing out would be very bad.

I fought to stay conscious as the last speck of faith I had in the human race shattered to the beat of the murderous child's footsteps as he casually walked away.

When my stomach stopped churning and my hands quit shaking, I crept out of my hiding spot. I gagged at the coppery-sweet smell of blood and tried not to notice the way the hunter's right foot twitched.

A blood curdling scream came from the direction the boy had gone, causing the hair on the back of my neck to raise. I shuddered, wondering if the scream came from the kid or another of his victims.

Within moments, the morning regained its quiet and my loneliness intensified. I ached for the camaraderie I used to find in the dark, understanding eyes, and big, velvety ears of my German shepherd. Kiana had been my best friend, my running partner, and my confidant. She was a great listener and the best roommate I'd ever had.

Her rationed food supply hadn't been enough and I couldn't bear to watch her starve. I didn't regret the decision to take her life. It had been the right thing to do. But during the lonely times, the selfish part of me wished I would have been a little more willing to let her suffer.

My sneakers assaulted the silence of the morning as they squeaked across dew softened grass. The city lay desolate and abandoned; no longer buzzing from the once constant hum of electricity and vehicle resonance. I took a deep, clean breath, longing for the stench of car exhaust and smog to fill my lungs. A door squeaked nearby. My chest constricted as I craved human contact, but feared the consequences. I kept walking.

In the stillness, his movement should have caught my eye, but I saw nothing. I experienced no premonition of being watched and heard no sound of his approach. Only the pressure of his left hand over my mouth alerted me to his presence, and by then it was too late.

Breathe.

His right hand trapped mine; pinning my dagger to my side, rendering it useless. My attacker's chest pressed against my back. Several inches taller than my 5'9" height, his mouth floated above my ear when he whispered, "Shh." Then, in one smooth motion his strong arms squeezed and lifted as he carried me into the bushes.

Too startled to struggle, the next thing I knew, I was balancing on my backpack with the weight of my assailant on top of me. His attention was elsewhere and the hand that covered my mouth loosened its grip. I took advantage of the slack and bit down hard on his middle finger.

"Don't!" he spat as he pulled his hand away. "You're gonna get us both killed if you don't hold still and be quiet." His whispers came between clinched teeth. "Shh. Here they come."

Confusion, more than anything, kept me silent. He'd passed up the chance to kill me, and he wasn't trying to rape me. His anxious heart pounded against my chest, as the scent of him invaded my senses; musk, wood smoke, metal, and sweat—comfortable and not at all unpleasant.

His whiskers scratched the side of my face when I tried to catch a glimpse of the man whose mass kept me pinned. But struggle as I might, all I could see was his chin and the hedge above him.

My patience wore out. I clenched my fists and was about to demand answers when I heard it: the unmistakable sound of someone or something approaching. My body went limp and my breathing grew shallow and hushed.

I know how to play this game.

"You're sure she went this way?" The whispered voice sounded male, coming from just a few feet away.

"Yes. But she was moving fast," came the feminine-sounding reply between deep breaths. "We'll catch her on the next block."

The slight squeak of their sneakers disappeared in the direction I had been heading, sending a shiver down my spine. I closed my eyes and searched for the image of the *Clue* board once more.

The living room is on the other side of the kitchen, but what is on the other side of the ballroom?

My rescuer adjusted his weight, allowing me to take a deep breath, and finally get a good look at him. Eyes the color of charcoal peered down at me under rugged, chin-length brown hair. His whiskers attempted to hide the faded scar that traced the outline of an otherwise perfect jaw. The left side of his mouth twitched up in a lop-sided smirk.

Sudden recognition of the man sped up my heart rate and dizzied me while time seemed to stop. I closed my eyes again; confident that the blackness I sought was much better than confirmation of who I was looking at.

"Connor Dunstan," I breathed his name. "You have got to be kidding me."

I could tell my response amused him by the vibration of his chest as he snickered.

I opened my eyes and stared at the cover-boy for all things corrupt and impious. I'd never actually met him, but everyone knew Connor. His face was plastered on the sides of buses, on park benches, and in commercials with slogans like, "At the law offices of Dunstan and Brayer, we'll help you get justice for your injustice." Justice ... right. Even before the fall of the US, the man I was currently pinned under had been a life-sucking, money-grubbing, ambulance-chasing, shady-deal-making fiend, aka personal injury attorney. And that had been while he was at his best. I had no desire to see him at his worst.

Connor Dunstan stood for everything I loathed.

My knife felt heavy.

My sister's family is dead and yet this? This is who you choose to let live?

"You okay?" Connor asked.

'Trust me. Trust him.' I felt the *call* respond.

I nodded, unwilling to commit to dialogue. Everything in my life balanced on a grey line. Connor was a greedy, heinous, detestable excuse for a human being, who had just saved my life. The world would be vastly less complicated if the bad guys could just be consistently loathsome.

Is that really too much to ask?

My muscles had started cramping when Connor stood and offered me his hand. I scowled at him and pushed myself up, refusing his assistance. Dagger clutched in my right hand, gun tucked in the back of my pants, I eyed him suspiciously.

Connor dismissed my scowling and eying, grabbed my left wrist, and started walking. I jerked my hand back, but his grip was tight and held firm.

"Where are you taking me?"

"Quiet. It's not safe to talk here." He pulled me behind him like some sort of puppy on a leash.

I considered reaching behind me for my gun, but I couldn't defy the *call*. When something consistently saves your life, you learn to just shut up and do what it tells you.

I really hope You know what You're doing.

Connor abruptly disappeared into the busted up window of a vandalized computer parts store. I scanned the area, preparing to make my escape, when his arms once again enclosed me and constricted my knife hand to my side.

This is getting old.

I kicked and writhed as he pulled me into a walk in safe, kicked the door closed behind us, and released me to spin the dial. By the time he turned to face me, I held my dagger within an inch of his throat.

"Give me one reason why I shouldn't kill you." I growled, angry that he'd successfully pulled off the same move on me twice.

"You don't know the combination. Kill me, and you're going to die in here." He glanced at me, glanced at the knife, and with all the cockiness of an overpaid, inflated attorney winked at me. "Now put that thing away before you hurt yourself."

My face burned as his indifferent attitude riled my temper. "You—"

"A simple thank you would suffice, you know." Connor leaned against the door to the safe.

"Thank you for what? Kidnapping me and shoving me into a ... a ... where are we anyway?" With my free hand I gestured to the room we occupied.

"I saved your life." He shrugged. "Do you think we could start over? Maybe even in a civilized manner?"

"You realize that's like asking me to break bread with Adolf Hitler?" I asked.

"Wow," he replied. "That has to be painful."

I raised an eyebrow at him in question.

"That stick, shoved so far up your—"

"Demon spawn." I took a step closer.

"Pretentious prude." He leaned toward me.

He was right. I mentally slapped myself for being so self-righteous. I was judging *him* with blood dripping from *my* hands. I studied Connor. No horns sprouted from his head, and he lacked the tail and pitchfork I'd always imagined he'd wield. In fact, had he been anyone else, I would have considered him handsome. Big, dark eyes with endless lashes, perfectly shaped masculine lips, and sexy-messy hair in all shades of brown.

Handsome but dangerous.

"Okay wise-guy. Enough with the pet-names. Just tell me what you want." I scoffed.

Connor looked me over as I searched the depths of his dark eyes. I dug my fingernails into my palms to remind myself that he was probably piercing my soul or something equally evil with that gaze.

He smiled and held his out his hand. "Let's start with your name."

4: Introductions

Liberty

"Liberty Collins. I'd shake your hand, but I'm terribly busy right now." I showed Connor my teeth and tapped his neck with the blade I held to it in affirmation.

He shrugged. "Liberty, eh? Mind if I call you Libby?"

I narrowed my eyes and moved the knife from his throat to his crotch. "Mind if I call you stubby?"

"Point taken." He held up his hands in surrender. "You're remarkably hostile, you know. You should probably see someone about that."

"I apologize." I flashed him another venomous smile. "I hate to sound cynical, but if I had a t-bone steak for every 'nice' person whose tried to kill me in the last three months, I'd need a weight loss clinic. I know about your flavor of 'justice,' and you're never gonna make Santa's nice list."

Connor opened his mouth to retaliate when a soft scuffing sound in the corner drew my attention. I glanced toward the noise to find a small girl sitting on the other side of a shelving unit. I did a double take, and then felt immediately embarrassed about the knife I was holding to Connor's nether regions. I raised my eyebrow and ever-so-smoothly restored the dagger to its rightful place at his throat.

"Mr. Dunstan, where are we? And who's the kid?" I nodded toward the child who was probably about ten, all elbows and knees. She sported Connor's shiny, brown hair, and her big, dark eyes were focused on the dagger, but she did not look concerned for my hostage. She raised her jaw, staring at me defiantly. The spirit in her eyes endeared me to her instantly.

Connor paused, his expression was a mask. I couldn't tell if he was about to kill me, or sell me oceanfront property in Arizona.

I pushed my knife a little closer to his throat. "Trust me or let me leave. Those are your only two options."

Connor looked at me thoughtfully.

"Decide, or you're gonna force me to do something we'll both regret."

He nodded resignedly, and introduced the girl. "My niece; Ashley. This is ... was my brother's store."

I looked to Ashley for her reaction, but she turned away.

"They're ... gone now. Asked me to take care of her." Connor gestured toward the girl.

"Alright. And so, what do you want from me?"

Connor sighed. "What? What do I want?"

I rolled my eyes. "Yeah. Why did you save me? Why am I here? What. Do. You. Want. From. Me?" It seemed an easy enough question and I couldn't understand why he was struggling with it. "You know, you seemed a lot smarter in the commercials."

The side of his mouth twitched. "Would you believe I'm looking for a chance at redemption?"

I blinked, and then burst into laughter. The idea of Connor Dunstan seeking redemption was hilarious. "Right." I said between fits of giggles. "And just yesterday I ran into Mother Theresa—she was looking for a biker bar."

His eyes grew guarded and hurt. "Am I so horrible that I'm beyond redemption?"

"No." I gulped. My inappropriate laughter left a sour taste in my mouth. In a world where everything had changed, I never should have assumed that Connor remained the same. No one is beyond redemption.

"It's by grace you are saved, not by your works." I quoted the words out of habit, and immediately regretted even opening my mouth.

"Grace?" Connor asked. "Grace from whom? From a God who has turned his back on the people he created?"

He snorted. "Open your eyes. If there was a God, would he allow his people to become ... this?"

I lowered my knife and took a step back, surprised by Connor's fervor.

"You think this is God's fault?" I shook my head. "That's rich. Exactly what I would expect from an attorney; blame someone else. You can't paddle away from the lifeboat, and then blame it when you drown."

Connor chuckled. "Great. Stuck with a religious nut."

"Religious nut?" I spat. "Stuck?"

The most annoying smirk spread across his face.

I raised an eyebrow at him. "A society without religion is like a vessel without a compass."

Connor's eyes widened. "Napoleon?"

I snorted. "I realize that this will probably defy all your beliefs about women, but yes, it is possible to have both; a chest, and brains."

Trust this infuriating man? What are You trying to do to me? Trust him? Are You sure?

I took a deep breath. "If you'd just open the door, I'll leave and you won't have to worry about being *stuck* with this *religious nut* any longer."

My body shook with anger and frustration. My face felt flushed, and my heart rate was dangerously fast.

I don't want to trust him. What I want to do is scratch out his eyeballs, throw him on the ground, and step on his throat to crush his larynx!

I took a step toward the door and reached for the handle.

"No." He held his arm in front of me.

"Excuse me?" I glared at him.

"No." He shook his head. "I'm not going to let you go out there and kill yourself. Too dangerous."

Manic laughter mixed with desperation and fear escaped from my mouth. "And you're going to prevent my death? I shook my head. "You? You're not exactly the white knight type, you know, so please forgive my doubt. There are enough enemies out there. I don't need to be *stuck* in a safe with one."

I'll show him stuck.

I clenched my fists. "By the way, if someone locks you in a safe against your will, they really shouldn't be allowed to refer to the experience as being *stuck* with you."

He sighed. "That might not have been the best word to use."

"You think?" My grip tightened around the dagger.

Why did my first interaction with another human being who wasn't trying to kill me or run from me have to be *this* man? He wasn't a human, he was a dog. No, my dog had been sweet and loving. Connor was more like a wolf, and I was no Little Red Riding Hood to be taken in by his smooth talking. Sure, he'd saved my life, but why? He was a big shot attorney. They never worked pro-bono, and it required more hope than I could muster to assume he had done anything out of the goodness of his heart.

I didn't need or want the company of a man who would stab me in the back. I just wanted to get to Canada, where I'd find Michelle and some semblance of a new life.

"This may come as a surprise to you but hey, I'm alive. I've survived without your help this far, and I'm pretty sure I don't need it now."

"I didn't mean for it to come out that way." He leaned back against the door to the safe.

"Please open the lock so I can leave." I could feel tears well up in my eyes. I was trapped and the walls were closing in on me, causing panic to cloud my judgment.

"No."

"Connor, let me out."

"No. Just listen ..."

"Please don't make me do this!" I pulled my dagger back up toward his throat. He grabbed my hand and in an impressive display of dexterity and speed spun me around so his chest pressed against my back and my arms were trapped beneath his own. I was bent at the waist, with Connor slumped over me.

Ashley's gasped. Her terrified face was in my direct line of sight. Her mouth hung open as she stared at us.

"Just listen to me for a minute, Libby ... Liberty. We can figure a way out of this." His breath brushed the side of my hair. "We have food. Our supplies have been adequate so far, but we can't hold out much longer here. Provisions are running thin. We're gonna have to leave soon."

Connor took a deep breath. He had me pinned. It was useless to struggle, so I didn't even try. If he wanted me dead, he'd had plenty of opportunities.

What does he want?

"What I propose ..." He stood up straight, pulling me with him. "Is that you eat with us now, and get some sleep."

"I don't—"

"You need food and sleep. And after you've rested if you still want to leave, you can. No questions asked."

Yeah right.

But the idea had definite appeal. My traitorous stomach growled at the suggestion of a meal. A few days ago all my food had been stolen, leaving me with only the pocket full of peanuts I'd eaten yesterday morning.

If I live through this I swear I'll never count calories again.

My stomach growled again and Connor smiled smugly.

I was too tired to fight and too hungry to disagree.

Let him kill me with a full stomach. I'll leave a huge mess for him to clean up.

I nodded and agreed to his terms. He released my arms and requested I sit and make myself comfortable. I lowered myself to the floor, took off my pack, and leaned against it.

Looking around, I had time to appreciate the shelter. It was kind of cozy, really. There was a dial lock on the outside and inside of the door that obviously did not require electricity. The air was a little stale, but circulated through small vents in the ceiling. There was a bucket in the corner which smelled faintly of urine, but the place was mostly clean and organized.

With the store surrounding it, the safe had double the protection against the elements. The day was still early, but the temperature was pleasant. Two sleeping bags were laid on top of twin air mattresses. Pillows and a wind-up flashlight topped each of the beds, and books were stacked in a corner.

There were a few supplies here and there, but the majority of the safe's shelves were empty, explaining Connor's concern.

The intoxicating scent of onions, peppers, and chili seasoning focused my attention back on Connor. "Mmm is that really chili?" I asked, as my mouth salivated. He put a small bowl of the spicy-scented ecstasy into my hands.

"Wow. You really know how to woo a girl, don't you?" I picked up the spoon and stirred the chili. Steam rolled off it, floating to my face, and torturing my growling stomach.

Connor flashed me his perfectly straight pearly-whites and handed Ashley a bowl. When she didn't acknowledge him, he placed it on the floor in front of her, and then sat down with his own across from me. She waited until he was seated before she picked up the bowl and started eating.

Okay, that's bizarre.

I filled the spoon with chili and lifted it to my lips. I didn't even test the heat, but opened my mouth and shoveled the warm food in. The spices danced over my taste buds as a warm, fuzzy sensation traveled down my throat and heated my stomach. I dismissed the spoon, picked up the bowl, and raised it to my mouth. Leaning back, I poured the spicy goodness down my throat, making all sorts of noises that should probably not be heard in public.

When I lowered my bowl, all eyes were on me. I wiped my sleeve over my mouth as Connor smirked. Ashley's eyes were wide as she watched me; her forgotten spoon full of chili hovered above her bowl.

"What?" I shrugged my shoulders. "I was hungry."

Ashley averted her eyes and continued eating. I tried desperately to think of some way to start a conversation with her, but what could I say?

How's school? See any good movies lately? So ... what do you want to be when you grow up? Hey you gonna eat that?

Right. Discouraged by inappropriate conversation topics, I defied the laws of nature and kept my mouth shut.

Connor had warmed the chili using a battery-generated hot plate and a small pot. When we were finished, he took the bowls and rinsed them in a bucket of water. He held a bottle of water toward Ashley, but she ignored him and he placed it in front of her. He tossed me a water and tidied up while I basked in the awkwardness of the situation.

What am I doing here?

Connor paused and studied me for a few moments. "The deal was for food and sleep. I'm gonna do some rounds and check on some things. I'll be gone at least four hours. Get some sleep."

He turned and walked toward the door. "When I get back, maybe we can talk for a minute before you go?" He spun the dial a few times, opened the door, and slipped out.

The lock spun from the outside, so I stood and jiggled the handle.

Yep. Locked in.

I sat on the floor, facing Ashley. "Well, looks like it's just you and me, kiddo."

She didn't climb onto my lap and beg me to sing her to sleep, but she didn't run away screaming either. My belly was more satisfied than it had been in several days and gravity pulled on my eyelids.

Maybe a few hours of sleep wouldn't be a bad thing.

Ashley watched me dubiously.

"Don't worry, Sweetie." I smiled. "I won't hurt you."

She picked up a book, walked over to one of the air mattresses, and sat down to read. I considered stretching out on the other mattress, but couldn't get past the creepiness of sleeping on Connor's bed. I already had enough nightmares.

Instead, I settled down on the floor, and made a makeshift pillow out of my jacket. My eyes closed as I focused on my life and its insane turn of events.

In literally ten months my life had went from wonderful to cataclysmic.

Twelve months ago the first "indestructible" company collapsed. In the months preceding that first failure, several struggling companies received assistance from the government. The economy had been steadily declining, and the government feared the catastrophic results of allowing these corporate giants to fold.

So Uncle Sam threw money at the businesses, hoping to plug the holes long enough for them to stabilize. Everyone said the recession wouldn't last forever, and the goal was to survive until it passed. So the once multi-billion dollar companies turned into taxpayer-subsidized, government-supervised, private companies. Unstable public/private hybrids, they were too public to make their own decisions, yet too private to be held accountable to the tax payers who'd become their lifeblood. Capitalism viewed them as monstrosities, and they were too anarchic for socialism.

Financial analysts wrung their hands as the national debt skyrocketed. No one knew the right course of action. The government watched as the hybrid companies bankrupted the nation, and unemployment rates broke records.

Next to plummet came the banks and other financial institutions. Already wounded by the big businesses reductions, they could not withstand the astronomical unemployment rates. People could no longer pay their mortgages, auto loans, and credit cards. Taxes weighed heavily upon the heads of a nation struggling to survive.

The few banks that endured were hesitant to lend, so money stopped flowing through free enterprise. Companies became insolvent, the stock market plummeted, banks were depleted, and the people starved.

Twelve months ago I was a young, bright professional reaching for the stars at a marketing firm in downtown Vancouver, Washington. According to my last review, I had overcome obstacles and proven myself to be a valuable team member. My boss was introducing me to the players, and helping me make the right contacts to grow my reputation. It was an amazing opportunity and I loved the challenges as well as the rewards.

Nine months ago it was a struggle to hold onto my job. Many of our clients had closed their doors, and desperation caused us to donate hours and hours of unclaimed overtime, just trying to keep the business afloat.

Six months ago I was in line at the unemployment office—my spirit broken and my hand out—praying for enough benefits to fill my empty cupboards. I had begun staggering payments for rent, insurance, and all the other bills I had accumulated during my success.

Three months ago the government officials disappeared and anyone receiving benefits woke up with empty bank accounts.

And now I'm locked in a safe with a little girl, awaiting the return of a questionable ally.

I should have run when I had the chance.

"Hey Ashley, can I ask you something?" I decided to pump the girl for information before I lost all consciousness.

She didn't answer, so I softened my words. "You don't have to answer me if you don't want ..."

I glanced at her, and she gave me another of her way-too-somber looks and nodded.

"What happened to your parents?"

Her eyes shifted back to her book. I was about to apologize for prying when she cleared her throat.

"Connor killed them."

5: Hardened

Connor

***Fort Lewis, Washington, June 8

A Latino man, dressed in fatigues, kneeled near the podium of the small Fort Lewis military chapel. Another Soldier approached hesitantly; stopping at the last pew, waiting to be addressed.

The kneeling man crossed himself, kissed the crucifix that hung around his neck, and stood up. "Report."

The Soldier saluted. "Excuse me Commander; we have word from the V Ranch."

A nod from the Commander encouraged him to continue.

"The Progression reached the ranchers two days before we did." *The Soldier clenched his fists and the vein in his forehead throbbed.*

The Commander exhaled, closed his eyes, and crossed himself again. "All dead?"

"Dead or taken." *The Soldier shifted his weight.* "We found a lot of bodies, but not as many as we expected."

The Commander nodded, and addressed the cross on the wall. "Recruited or escaped?"

***

I closed and locked the safe door behind me, letting out a deep breath.

Can't believe I'm leaving Ashley with that nut-job.

My hand reached for the dial.

No, someone that self-righteous wouldn't hurt a child.

I stared at the door as the minutes ticked away. There were no sounds of violence; no blood came pooling under it.

This is ridiculous. She's your only chance of getting Ashley out of that safe. Don't blow it.

I walked away, knowing I'd be the subject of conversation on the other side of the door. I left Jacob's store at a jog; determined to run off some tension. I was getting nowhere with Liberty. Maybe Ashley would have better luck.

Women.

As I ran, my mind floated back to the last woman I'd been with; the blonde reporter from NBS. I met her at a quaint Japanese lounge on Broadway. I arrived first and requested a secluded table in the corner. The lights were dimmed and the fragrance from the purple orchid centerpiece added to the ambiance.

She beamed as she approached the table, wearing a fitted, knee-length blue dress that brought out her eyes. Her legs looked stunning in the matching heels, and when I widened my eyes, she dimpled.

"You look ... amazing." I stood and took her hand.

She blushed. "Thank you. And you." She gestured at my black on black Armani. "But Connor Dunstan always looks slick."

I smiled as we sat.

The waiter approached and handed us each a menu. "Can I get you started with something from the bar?"

My date differed to me and I smiled, approvingly.

"Ginjo Sake."

The sushi was exquisite, the Sake was light and clean, and the night was magical.

"About these allegations ..." She smiled wickedly in an attempt to bring the case into our easy conversation.

"Ah, ah, ah." I twitched my finger back and forth. "No business before the third glass of Sake." I picked up my glass and offered a toast. "To a gorgeous woman, and the beginning of a beautiful relationship."

She dimpled again and tapped her glass to mine.

With business effectively put on the back burner, we drank and talked for hours.

She glanced at her watch. "It is getting late. I should probably call a cab."

The corner of my mouth twitched.

Predictable.

"Absolutely not."

She smiled, no doubt thinking I was predictable as well.

"I drove. I'll take you home."

She batted her lashes. "I don't want to be a bother. I can call a cab."

She reached for her cell phone and I put my hand over hers. "It's no trouble at all," I insisted. This was a dance, and I knew the steps well.

I paid the bill, tipped the valet, and then slid the compliant little blonde into my SUV.

"I was planning on heading to the office after I drop you off. Do you mind if we swing by my house for my briefcase?" I led my partner into another spin of the intricate steps.

"Of course, I would love to see your place." She smiled as I turned over the engine.

Sandy? Sadie? Stacy? Shirley? I should probably start writing down their names.

I winced as my thoughts turned back to the temperamental red-head who'd just held a knife to my throat: Liberty

Maybe redemption is overrated.

Somehow I ended up back at the remains of Jacob's house. After mentally degrading my feet, I conceded to the ritual and grabbed a handful of ash.

"We're leaving, Jacob. We can't stay here any longer." I whispered the words into the wind.

My eyes were beginning to water when I heard gravel crunch behind me. I grabbed the gun out of my pocket and spun around. A skinny, dark-haired woman stood before me. She held out her hands and her lips stretched into a smile that could only be described as unnatural.

"I didn't mean to startle you." She took a cautious step forward. "What happened here? Do you need help?"

She's approaching me? Alone?

I kept my gun aimed at her chest. "Don't come any closer."

Her sinister smile widened. "Oh honey, I'm not the one you have to worry about."

My peripheral vision caught the movement to my right. I shifted my weight to my left foot, spun right, and fired my Glock at the approaching figure. My bullet entered his stomach. He staggered, and then continued the motion he'd begun, attempting to bring the tire iron in his hand down on my head. I ducked and stepped back as it whizzed by my ear.

The woman scratched at my face. I stepped back, but her claws sunk into my cheek. My right hand rose in an attempt to block her, but she grabbed it and grappled with me for the gun.

With my left hand I grabbed the tire iron and pulled the man closer, so he couldn't swing at me. I bent my elbow and raised it quickly, making contact under of the woman's chin. The blow threw her head back, causing her to cough and struggle for breath.

The man's strength faded with his coloring. He lunged at me in one last, feeble swing, and then collapsed. The woman wobbled over and sat beside him.

"Larry, honey, wake up." His glossed over eyes stared back at her. She felt for a pulse, and then glared at me. "You killed him!"

I let out a breath and looked down at myself. My stomach was covered in the man's blood and my pants were torn. I turned and walked away.

"You killed Larry! You can't just leave me here alone."

I took another step.

"Murderer!"

Keep walking.
I heard the rustle of footsteps as others approached her.
"No, get away! Someone help!"
Don't look back.
"Help! Please some—"
'And the goblins'll get ya if you don't watch out.'

6: Decisions

Liberty

My eyes widened at Ashley's revelation. Surprise, confusion, anger, outrage; my emotions spiraled out of control as her dark eyes locked on mine. The anguish and truth they revealed could not be denied. My heart broke for the pain I could see burned into her features. My soul wept for hers.

"Killed them? Connor killed your parents?" The guy—no matter how repulsive he'd been in the past—had just saved my life. Slime ball—yes, but murderer?

She nodded.

I closed my eyes.

Is this what I'm supposed to do? Save this little girl from her uncle?

She hadn't called him "Uncle Connor," but maybe family titles are lost when you kill your relatives?

And I thought my family had problems.

I digested the news, waiting for her to elaborate, but she was apparently done talking about the subject.

"Do you know the code to the door?" I opened my eyes and watched her.

She shook her head.

Well then, nothing to do but wait.

I was exhausted. Ashley's announcement should have woken me up, but it didn't. Even the knowledge that her homicidal uncle was coming back couldn't override the heaviness of my eyelids. I felt like a horse; rode hard and put away wet, and I needed sleep.

"Okay, I'm gonna get some rest then. Please wake me the second you hear him approach?"

Ashley nodded again—she wasn't big on words.

Sleep had almost overcome me when her mousy, sweet voice pleaded, "Please, don't leave me here with him."

I sighed. This was not what I wanted, but there was no way I could deny the plea of a scared little girl. I cracked my eyes. Ashley stared at me like I was Wonder Woman, come to save the day.

"I promise," I replied as my eyes closed. Then I prayed for indestructible bracelets and an invisible airplane.

***

'Get out ... NOW!'

The mental command was urgent and demanding as it interrupted my sleep. I'd been dancing with my eighth grade crush when the call *woke me from my dream and compelled me to evacuate the tent. Normally a still, small voice, the* call's *intensity was suddenly like a fire alarm, driving away all thoughts of sleep.*

I searched around our dark, flimsy, nylon shelter until I found Michelle. "Wake up, Shell," I pleaded, but she was sound asleep.

'**Drag her! Do it now!**' *the* call *became a compulsion; so powerful it was excruciating. I felt like I would spontaneously combust if I didn't get out of the tent, but I knew I couldn't leave my friend behind.*

I unzipped the flap, grabbed Michelle by the shoulders, and dragged her toward the outline of the large canvas tent where her dad—Howard—slept. My shaking fingers fumbled with the little metal zipper.

'NOW! NOW! NOW!'

The thoughts battered my body like physical blows. I bit down on my lip until I tasted blood, trying to pull myself together.

"Dad," I pleaded. "Help me, I can't ..." Howard wasn't my dad, but he was the closest thing I'd ever had to one. I'd given him the title when Michelle and I became best friends in kindergarten.

The inside of the tent suddenly lit up like a beacon of hope. I started sobbing. Safety was so close: visible yet unattainable.

"What is it? What's happened to Michelle?" Howard frantically unzipped the flap and helped me drag her still sleeping form inside it.

"Nothing ... with Michelle." I huffed, trying to catch my breath. "But something's wrong." I wiped my nose with my sleeve. "I don't know what, but I just—I just—"

Then we heard it: the very eerie, very loud, very close, scream of a cougar.

There are few things in life more terrifying than the sound of a cougar. Not something one could get used to, it's like woman's scream laced with malice, dripping with hatred. The hair on the back of my neck stood up and I instantly needed to use the restroom.

The scream woke up Michelle. I clutched her hand and we scrambled to the back of the tent. Terrified, we clung to each other, and our fear was a thick fog, clouding up the tent.

Howard grabbed his Marlin .22 caliber, bolt-action rifle—our hunter's safety training weapon. He slept with it loaded beside him while we were camping, and I suddenly understood why.

Howard held the rifle in one hand and pulled back the unzipped tent flap with the other. The darkness outside was sinister and evil, waiting for a victim to claim. He raised his shotgun and bravely stepped into the night.

A reverberating crack echoed throughout the valley ...

***

"Wake up, he's here."

When I opened my eyes I found Ashley kneeling beside me, whispering into my ear. The sound of the spinning dial washed over me like a bucket of cold water, rinsing away the lingering dream residue.

"The food, Ash—" I glanced at the shelves; only a few cans of lima beans remained.

She patted her backpack. "Already done."

I nodded, impressed by her forethought. Then the magnitude of the situation hit me. What would we have to do to get out of here alive? Would he fight us? Would I have to kill him?

Breathe. You can do this. He's a murderer.

By the time Connor opened the door and stepped inside, I was standing behind it with my gun drawn. I closed the door for him—I'm considerate like that—and instructed him not to move.

Holding his arms up in surrender, he didn't look surprised to see the weapon in his face. "What now?" His gaze drifted from me to Ashley.

"No. My gun, my questions. Did you kill Ashley's parents?" I glared at him, aiming toward ferocious, but feeling more like a scared puppy than a frightening lion.

He took a deep breath. "Liberty, let me explain—"

"No. You don't get to explain. Just. Answer. The. Question. Did you kill Ashley's parents? Your brother and his wife?" I was unsuccessful at keeping the disdain from my voice.

"Things are ... complicated." He took a step closer to Ashley.

I inched forward and put my gun against his chest. "Really? Because they sure aren't very complicated from here. Did you kill them or not?"

"Ash—" His big, dark eyes sought the girl, but she turned away, and walked behind me.

"No. You talk to me." I nudged his chest with the barrel, noticing the smear of blood down the front of his shirt and the scratches on his cheek.

He didn't look like that when he left, did he?

"What's with the blood?" I gestured at his shirt. "Do you just go around killing people?"

He blinked at me, and then looked down at his shirt. "Um ..."

"Forget it. We're leaving. Do *not* follow us." I motioned for Ashley to go ahead of me. I stepped out of the safe and pushed on the door, but Connor blocked it with his foot, and holding it slightly ajar.

He stared into my eyes, making me wonder if he'd let us leave without a fight. I glared back and he took a deep breath.

"Promise me you'll be careful with her."

I hiked my pack higher on my shoulders, preparing for a fast escape. "I'm not the one who killed her parents."

His charcoal eyes were still locked on mine as he removed his foot from the door and stepped back. I closed the safe, spun the dial, grabbed Ashley's hand, and fled.

Over the next few days, we cautiously made our way out of the city, heading east. At night, we'd pull out the sleeping bags and snuggle close for warmth in whatever abandoned building we could find. Ashley was quiet and reserved. I seldom heard a peep from her and never a complaint. We walked for long periods of time in companionable silence, rarely filling the quiet with meaningless chatter.

The miles were long and tiring, the ground was hard and cold, but the company was nice. She was strong for her size and fast for her age; a city girl who loved to watch the wildlife frolic, and marvel at the beauty of nature. Her presence was tremendously comforting after so many months of paranoia induced solitude.

Her innocent smiles chased away my nightmares, and her dependence necessitated my sanity.

***June 13

Early in the morning of our fifth day since leaving Connor we came across a modest farm northeast of Alderton. As we approached, memories of my family's happy farmhouse amplified the wrongness of this one. An unnatural quiet pined for the baying of livestock and the sounds of their caretakers. A tractor sat, neglected and forlorn, waiting to be of use once again. I waited and listened, but the creepy Twilight Zone music never started playing.

Farms are supposed to be life. This is death.

Petrified cow dung was evidence that the corral we walked through once held cattle, but had been empty for a time. The front door hung askew and we approached cautiously. Marks of forced entry scratched up the frame. The all too familiar *parfum de la mort* was heavy on the air, so I drew my gun as we entered the house.

The home was a recently updated seventies ranch-style. The large, open family room we stepped into would have passed for cheerful if mom, pop and the two young boys hadn't been rotting in the center of the room.

I plugged my nose and averted my eyes, but could still hear the sounds of maggots crawling over their dead bodies.

"Ash, don't look." I held out my hand like it could block her view.

Of course she didn't listen. She glanced at the center of the room, and immediately started gagging. While she ran outside to be sick I grabbed the afghan off the couch and spread it over the family. Wrists still bound together, they'd died facing each other in a circle.

I didn't investigate the bodies further. The small glimpse I'd had was enough to churn my stomach and add to my ever increasing collection of nightmares. I crossed myself and wished the family peace. The blanket didn't block the rancid odor, but at least we couldn't see their hollow eye sockets anymore. Ashley joined me when she was done outside, and we tried not to breathe while we continued toward the kitchen.

The pantry had been thoroughly ransacked, but the thieves had overlooked the canisters sitting on the counter. I found flour, sugar, pancake batter, and cornmeal in the partially full containers. I dumped each treasure into its own plastic baggie and shoved them into my pack.

Further exploration of the kitchen revealed a can of non-stick spray, various seasonings and a small bottle of maple flavoring, all of which I took. I grabbed a cast-iron skillet and handed it to Ashley. She looked at me like I was crazy.

"Put it in your bag. We'll need it tonight and it can be used as a weapon in a pinch."

I could see the question in her eyes, so I mocked hitting someone over the head with the pan. She stifled a giggle at my ridiculous pantomime, and stuffed the pan into her bag.

We exited through the back door, and slipped into the small building on the side. I rummaged around for a fishing pole—didn't find one—but didn't come away empty handed either. Fishing line, hooks, and some of those scissors that can cut through anything all found their way into my pack.

"Move over MacGyver." I zipped up the bag and returned it to my shoulders.

Ashley looked at me questioningly. "Who's MacGyver?"

I shook my head. "Who's MacGyver? Only the most amazing genius-crime-fighter ever. He never carried a gun, and constantly saved the day using only his vast scientific knowledge and the items he had on hand."

She rolled her eyes, which only encouraged me to continue. "He built bombs out of things like bubble gum. You seriously don't know who MacGyver is? Did you even watch TV?"

Ashley cast me one of those apprehensive looks usually reserved for religious fanatics and door-to-door salesmen. "Mom wasn't big on violence."

"MacGyver wasn't violent." I leaned against the counter. "He was a genius." I held up my hands. "It was educational."

By the time we left the farm, I felt much better about our chance of survival. We headed more north than east to shoot the gap between Puyallup and Enumclaw. I planned to stay east of Highway 167, to avoid as many towns and people as possible without drifting too far off course.

The map in my back pocket advertised several little lakes, streams, and rivers, which we could use as water sources along the way. The weather had been mostly dry and we'd need to fill up our water bottles soon.

About three more hours of walking brought us to the enchanting sounds and smells of a small stream. We approached with practiced caution before descending upon the water source. An abundance of animal tracks marked the spot as a popular watering hole.

"See this Ash?" I pointed at the ground before me.

She nodded.

"Deer track."

She studied the ground. "How can you be so sure?"

"Size and shape." I pointed to the deer droppings a few feet away. "That helps too."

She wrinkled her nose. "What about this one?" She pointed to a small paw print.

I considered the track. The claw marks were faint— definitely canine. "Most likely a wolf," I replied. "Or maybe a wild dog."

"There are wolves out here?" Ashley looked around suspiciously.

"Of course. But don't worry; they have plenty to eat in the early summer. They won't bother us."

I owed much of my survival to my outdoor packed childhood. Michelle's father—Howard—had been the local butcher in our home town. He was a widower, and Michelle was his entire world. Positively the coolest dad I ever met, he welcomed me along on their escapades. An avid outdoor enthusiast, Howard served as our self appointed camping, fishing, hunting and hiking guide. He was always more than willing to drag us into the safety of Mother Nature and away from the dangers of boys.

When we forgot to "moan and groan," about the lack of comforts in the wilderness, we actually enjoyed ourselves. He taught us the dangers and benefits of his natural playground with never ending enthusiasm. I grew up traipsing around the forest after him with Michelle by my side. He never gave up on our wilderness training, and I was grateful now more than ever.

Without the things he had taught me, I would have perished months ago.

I rummaged through the tall grass until I found a decently strong stick; about three feet long. Ashley sat and rifled through her pack as I removed excess branches and leaves. She watched me from the corner of her eye.

After unrolling a length of fishing line, I cut it and tied one end securely around the stick. To the other end, I attached a hook. A small rock toward the hook end of the line acted as a weight and completed my handiwork.

I dug around in the soft bank until I found a very large worm. I cut it in half and stuck the hook through one side.

Ashley made a sound of disgust. I raised an eyebrow at her, and she returned her attention to her pack.

Now that the hook was properly baited, I cast my line and sat down to wait. The sound of water rushing over rocks soothed my mind. The clean scents and tranquil sounds assaulted the tense muscles in my neck and back, forcing me to relax. I closed my eyes and reveled in the warmth of the sun against my eyelids.

A shadow appeared, blocking my sunshine. "That is not a fishing pole."

I chuckled and opened my eyes. Ashley had her arms crossed and brows furrowed as she scrutinized my work.

"You don't even know who MacGyver is. What exactly do you *think* you know about fishing poles?"

She eyed the pole. "I've seen them before. They don't look like ... like that."

"Yes, but have you ever seen a 'custom built' fishing pole?" I nodded toward the stick in my hands.

She stared at me like I was thick for a moment, and then sat down.

"You can really catch fish with that?" Her expression changed from doubtful to curious.

"People have been catching fish since long before fishing poles were invented." I felt something exploring the worm on my line, and waited patiently as the top of the pole bobbed with the nudges.

Finally, the slack pulled tight. Ashley gasped as I jerked the line up and to the left, pulling the fish out of the water and dangling it over the ground.

I lowered the pole and ran over to inspect our catch—Ashley hot on my heels. It was a large, healthy rainbow trout. Colorful scales reflected the fading sunlight as it flapped around in the grass. Using my dagger, I removed the hook from the trout's gill and went to retrieve the other half of the worm to try my luck again.

I cast the line back in and sat on the bank.

I don't mean to sound greedy, but ... um ... any more in there?

"Wow," Ashley said when she finally came back to life. She regained her seat next to me with eyes the size of silver dollars. "That was so cool. I can't believe you caught a fish on a stick!"

A smile spread across my face as I offered her the pole. "Wanna try?" She looked at me and shook her head.

"Come on Ash, it's actually fun."

I handed her the pole and she griped it tightly. Her entire body looked stiff.

"Relax," I encouraged. "This is supposed to be the lazy person's sport."

She giggled and loosened up.

"I used to fish a lot, you know. When I was your age ..." I snickered at myself for sounding like an old lady. "My best friend, Michelle, and I went fishing with her father often. We'd only hold our poles for about thirty minutes before we'd grow bored and 'accidentally fall in' the water so we could go swimming."

She glanced at the stream. "Isn't it freezing?"

"It's only cold for the first few minutes." I shrugged. "You get used to it quickly."

Ashley was starting to squirm when her line went taut. She stared at the pole as I watched her expression. Her eyes lit up and the smile that spread across her face was precious.

I helped her jerk the pole up and snag the trout.

"You did it! Your first fish, Ash!"

When her blush wore off, she bore her satisfaction like a gold medal, beaming a smile that would make Mona Lisa proud.

Between the two of us we caught two more trout in the next half hour. Then I taught Ashley to gut and clean them properly.

As she brought the skillet out of her backpack I searched the area and gathered twigs, grateful for the dry weather. I hardly ever chanced a fire, but it was still light out and the idea of fried trout was making me giddy. The area was heavily wooded, with lots of trees to hide us, and it wouldn't take long to cook our small catch. We would be fed and long gone before nightfall.

The fish were happily sizzling in spray butter and a small amount of seasonings I'd found in my pack when I heard an unfamiliar cough. I looked up to find a large, grimy, disturbingly hairy man with a knife held to Ashley's throat.

"Mm fish." He leered at me and licked his lips like, "Mm woman."

How did I not hear him approach? Stupid. Need to pay attention.

Ashley's look of terror pulled me from my self-deprecating thoughts, and made me strangely calm. I glanced at the pack that held my gun; useless. My knife was equally worthless, lying by the river, where we'd used it to gut fish.

Um ... Help?

"What do you want?" I put on my best helpless façade, batting my eyes and trembling; going for an Emmy.

The newcomer showed his repulsive yellow teeth in a predatory smile that made my skin crawl. "Well, let's start with some dinner and then we can talk about dessert." He looked me over.

Bile rose as I tried not to think too much on the insinuation.

His eyes lingered on my chest. "Two pretty, young ladies out here all alone, bet you ladies are lonely."

It took a conscious effort not to roll my eyes while I considered the workings of the amazingly vast male ego. But he was armed, so I did what women have been doing for years; disarmed him with the most charming smile in my arsenal and lied.

"Absolutely. You should put down the knife and join us. We've had no one to talk to in so very long."

Was that really a southern drawl in my voice?

I swallowed ideas about women's rights and equality and ignored the sound of every woman in my lineage rolling over in her grave as I batted my lashes. All that mattered was Ashley. And as the man withdrew his knife and set her aside, my heart did a back-flip.

He paused and narrowed his eyes; his big paw tightened around Ashley's arm and she winced. "Promise you won't try anything or the girl here dies."

Hoping he wasn't smarter than I'd assumed, I held up my hands in surrender and tried to look submissive. It was a stretch, but I'd taken classes.

And Momma thought drama was just an easy "A".

"Of course. What could we possibly do to you? You'd kill us." My cheeks were cramping from smiling so long.

The stranger reeked of old cigarettes, beer and sweat. He sat next to me, putting his hand inappropriately high on my thigh. I smiled at him through clenched teeth.

Enjoy it now buddy, it won't last.

The two large, flat stones I'd previously washed in the stream to use as plates were on the ground beside the man. I stood and reached for one.

He held up his knife warningly. "Slowly."

I winked like we were sharing some secret innuendo. He smiled back and lowered his knife.

I placed all four of the trout on the makeshift plate and handed them to him with my left hand. My peripheral vision caught sight of a shadowy figure quickly moving out of the bushes, toward the stranger. As the stranger turned to see what had caught my eye, I grabbed the still sizzling skillet and lunged forward, bashing him over the head with it.

He toppled over as Connor withdrew his knife from the stranger's back.

7: Family

Connor

*** *Fort Lewis, Washington, June 13*

A sharp rap on the door of the Commander's small apartment woke the man sleeping inside. He climbed out of bed, wrapped his bathrobe around himself, and hurried to the door. Unlocking the chain, he pulled it open to see a Soldier standing on his doorstep.

He sighed, knowing the news couldn't possibly be good. "Report."

The Soldier saluted. "Yessir. Jacobson has returned."

The Commander's eyebrows rose in surprise. "Jacobson? And the team?"

"No sir. Just Jacobson."

The Commander closed his eyes and crossed himself. He took deep breaths, in through the nose, out through the mouth. "Has Captain Parkins been notified?"

***

Liberty and I sized each other up. Our chests rose and fell as we each enjoyed an adrenaline high. Liberty's frying pan-wielding proficiency was impressive, but she looked completely startled by my presence.

Someone needs to pay closer attention …

"I won't let you hurt her!" Ashley yelled at me as she ran between us.

"Do you really think I would, Ash?" I stared into her accusatory eyes and saw exactly what she thought I was capable of.

Will she hate me forever?

"Libby is all I have. I won't let you kill her too." Her jaw thrust stubbornly outward, reminding me of a pit-bull.

"You were following us this entire time?" Liberty's brows knit together. "And when you saw we were in danger you what ... rushed in to knife the guy and save the day?"

I shrugged, leaned over, and wiped my knife on the dead man's shirt. Then I bent down and checked his pockets.

"What are you doing?" Liberty sounded appalled.

My hand ran across something hard. I reached in, retrieved a lighter, and shook it; half full. I handed it to Liberty. "What do you think I'm doing? I'm seeing if he has anything we need."

"You can't steal from him! He's dead!" She stared at the lighter and shook her head. "I don't want that!"

"It's not like he's going to use it." I shoved it in my pocket.

"You—you—why did you kill him?"

"What?" I shook my head. "He was—"

She held up the frying pan. "I had the situation under control."

"How was I supposed to know that?" I stood and walked toward the stream.

Can't win no matter what I do.

Liberty wouldn't let it go. "We didn't ask for your help."

I stopped and faced her. "Dammit, Liberty, I promised my brother I would take care of his daughter."

"Oh." She raised her eyebrows. "The brother you murdered?"

I clenched my teeth and turned away from her, taking my pack off my back and unzipping it as I took a step.

Refill the water and get out.

Then it hit me: Ashley had spoken to me for the first time in months. Albeit it was more of an angry yell, but there were words involved. I stopped and stared at her, as my pack dangled from my hand.

She did speak to me. Could it be possible? Would she finally listen?

"Ash?"

Her eyes landed on mine for a split second before she turned away.

I stepped toward her. "Would you just hear me out? Please? Let me explain?"

She paused, looking at the ground.

Am I getting through?

"I loved them too." I put my hand on her shoulder. "You're all *I* have. Please don't shut me out."

Her shoulders tensed as she moved away. With her back still facing me her voice was quiet, controlled, and dripping with disgust when she finally spoke. "Don't touch me. Don't talk to me. Don't even look at me. I. Hate. You."

I closed my eyes and received her anger as each word ripped through me. I deserved it. I killed her parents. Over and over I relived the last words I spoke to my brother.

'No, Jacob, don't ask this of me.'

I felt Ashley move. I couldn't open my eyes; didn't want to see her walking away from me again.

She hates me.

"I'm sorry." I muttered the words and opened my eyes in time to see Ashley disappear behind a tree. I picked up my pack and, with my head down, headed for the stream. Liberty's shoes appeared in my view.

Great.

I turned my angle to walk around her, but she blocked me. Sensing the inevitable, I looked up at her face. Her expression was different; confused. She studied me in the same way I sized up new clients; evaluating their honesty, determining their level of commitment.

"Connor, look—"

I stopped her, holding up my hand. "No, I get it. I'm just gonna refill my water, and I'll be on my way." I pulled the bottles out of my pack as I walked.

Liberty put her hand in front of me, palm facing upward.

My brows knit together.

She sighed. "Hand me a couple of the bottles. I'll help." When I didn't immediately do as she requested, she took two bottles out of my hand and started walking toward the stream, stopping when I didn't follow. "Coming?"

I didn't want to. I wanted to be alone, but I was getting used to doing things I didn't want to.

"Um ... I may have been a bit harsh." Liberty filled up one of the bottles, screwed on the lid, and handed it to me. "It's just that I hate to see a child hurting. Kinda gives me this crazy-protective vibe." She lowered the next bottle into the stream and glanced at me.

I crouched down and started filling the bottles. "She never gave me the chance to explain. Every time I'd try, she'd stick her fingers in her ears and start singing."

Why am I telling her this?

"I'm just so ... I don't know what to do." I twisted the plastic lid too tightly and it cracked. "Damn."

Liberty's stare was uncomfortably intense as her green eyes seemed to penetrate my soul.

"You cannot be rebuilt, until you are destroyed."

What the—? How can she—?

The bottle slipped out of my hand. I reached for it as the fast current swept it away. I disregarded the lost bottle and stared at Liberty. "What? What did you just say?"

She bit her lip and looked down into the water.

Did she know Jacob? Is there some kind of book they get these sayings out of?

"Nothing. Never mind." She handed me the last full bottle, stood, and raised an eyebrow at me. "Why did you do it?" I started to speak, but she interrupted me. "No. On second thought, you can explain it to both of us."

I let out an exasperated breath. "I've tried. She won't listen."

"Then you haven't tried hard enough."

There were so many thoughts jumbled in my mind that I couldn't force any of them through my lips. My confusion must have been evident, because Liberty rolled her eyes.

"Eat with us. You get *one chance* to plead your case, Counselor." She narrowed her eyes. "And if you mess with me, or hurt that little girl, I swear I will cut out your spleen."

"Why my spleen?"

"Because—" A vicious smile spread across her face. "You *could* live without it."

By the time I'd replenished my water supply and washed up, the girls had the fire out and were ready to go. Liberty handed us each a fish and we were on our way, munching as we walked.

The crispy skin and flaky meat danced over my taste buds. Liberty moaned, and I felt the corner of my lips twitch. She glared at me and licked her fingers.

She handed the fourth fish to Ashley, who gave part of it back.

"You're a good kid, Ash." Liberty messed with Ashley's hair as the girl swatted her hand away. They giggled and wrestled, wiping greasy hands on each other. I smiled in spite of myself.

Liberty split the remaining half of the fish, handing part of it to me.

I looked her over. "Keep it. You need it worse than I do."

"What's that supposed to mean?" She was looking at me and stumbled, but steadied herself.

My mouth twitched. "You're nothing but skin and bones."

She smiled. "I think that's the nicest thing you've said to me. Now take the damn thing. If I end up any more in your debt I'm going to throw myself from a cliff."

I chuckled and took the fish, afraid she'd shove it down my throat if I didn't.

We walked in silence until the sky darkened. I'd tried to get Ashley to hear me out for so long, and now that I had the opportunity I found myself procrastinating. No amount of talking would undo what I'd done, and I didn't want to take the chance that my explanation would make things worse. The unsaid words hung over our heads like a dark cloud; ominous and foreboding.

"Look." Liberty stopped and stood beside me. "I'm so not comfortable with this situation. We made a deal." She crossed her arms. "Start talking."

I held up my arms in surrender, and then collapsed on the ground. "Okay, okay."

We were exhausted; physically and emotionally. Liberty sat down across from me and Ashley sat next to her, looking everywhere except at me.

I pulled up a handful of grass and broke the blades into small sections as I told the tale. "Jacob was diagnosed with type-one diabetes when he was young. Since then, he's been insulin dependent, but the doctors have never really been able to control his blood sugars. His levels spiked and plummeted often."

Liberty whispered to Ashley and the girl nodded.

"We needed some clean clothes and supplies, so Jacob and I decided to head to the house leaving his wife, Cathy, with Ashley in the safe. Soon after we arrived, Jacob became disoriented and shaky. I'd seen the signs before, and knew he needed sugar, but I thought we had more time.

I went up the stairs ahead of him, and had just stepped into Ashley's room when I heard several loud thumps. I ran to the top of the stairs and found Jacob lying at the bottom; having a seizure."

Liberty's hand went to her mouth. "A boy I played softball with had a seizure on the pitching mound during one of our games. Pretty scary stuff."

I locked eyes with Liberty, anxious to see if she how she'd judge me for what I'd done. "As if the seizure wasn't enough, he broke his leg in the fall."

Ashley looked at me with wide eyes. She'd seen her father's seizures. I closed my eyes and remembered my brother; every muscle contracting, jerking on the floor.

"I moved him into bed and set the bone, but couldn't do much else. He came out of the seizure, but was still shaking, sweating, and unresponsive. I'd just elevated his leg when Cathy showed up. We'd been gone too long, and she and Ashley had gotten worried. She'd talked Ashley into staying behind, but none of us knew how long that would last. We never should have given Ash the code."

Liberty squeezed Ashley's shoulders, but the kid continued to stare at me.

"There was no food left in their house, so Cathy insisted on running to the neighbor's to see if she could find any. I told her it was too dangerous, but she wouldn't listen." I stared into the distance, remembering the sounds outside their house; gunshots, shouts, crying. "People were already acting crazy. The city sounded like a warzone. But once Cathy made up her mind about something, there was no changing it.

Jacob started talking to me, finally sounding lucid, right before Cathy came stumbling back into the room. She was holding her side, and her shirt and jeans were soaked in blood—too much blood. I tried to get a look at the wound, but she pushed my hands away, and staggered into bed, wrapping herself in Jacob's arms."

"She was bleeding?" Liberty looked confused. "What happened to her?"

I shrugged. "I don't know. Shot? Stabbed? She'd gotten away somehow. There wasn't time to get the details. The commotion outside was nearing."

"So you killed them to save your own skin?" She shook her head.

"No!" I broke all the blades of grass remaining in my hand, tossed them aside, and pulled up some more. Then I took a deep breath. "My brother asked me to kill him and his wife." My voice cracked, and I cleared my throat. "And when I declined, he begged me."

Jacob's request still haunted me.

'You must. It's the only way.'

'No Jacob, don't ask this of me. I can't kill you!'

'Yes you can. And you have to. Ashley's life depends on it.'

Liberty reached out her hand, placing it on my shoulder.

"Liar," Ashley spat, getting to her feet. "You lie! They wouldn't leave me! They wouldn't just give up. Mom always said you were a good liar."

Yes, but not this time.

Liberty stood and went to Ashley, wrapping her arms around the girl.

I watched them; wishing Ashley would let *me* comfort her. "I didn't know what to do." I felt the hopeless tears slide down my cheeks. "He was right. We were out of options. Cathy was dying. And even if he would have left her behind, there was no way I could've gotten him back to the safe with his broken leg."

I looked at Ashley, who was seething at me. "More than even their own lives, they wanted you to survive. They loved you so much, that they never even hesitated."

Her small frame shook from her sorrow. I glanced at Liberty who was running her fingers through Ashley's hair, while watching me. She sniffed and wiped away a tear.

'Please, Con, kill me. Save her.'

My chest constricted.

'No, Jacob, don't ask this of me.'

8: Behavior

Liberty

"Ash, I'm so sorry." I squeezed her shoulders as the child mourned for her parents.

I unzipped my pack, pulled out Frog the stuffed bear, dusted him off, and presented him to Ashley. Frog stared at her with his one glossy, black eye; begging to be accepted.

"Frog, this is Ashley," I introduced them. "Frog once belonged to someone dear to me. He hates being locked away in my smelly pack and complains continuously. I'd really appreciate it if you took him off my hands."

She rolled her eyes.

I shrugged and pulled open the flap of my bag. "Alright, back in the pack you go. Might want to plug your nose."

Her soft, small hand grabbed mine. "It wouldn't hurt to hang out with him for a little bit. You know, see if we're compatible."

I fought to hide my smile.

She studied the bear's battered appearance. "Who did he belong to?" Her delicate fingers explored the Band-Aid on his arm and the empty spot where his missing eye should be.

Frog was flawed and rough-looking, but he was exactly what Ashley needed. She'd love him regardless of his imperfections.

"My niece, Megan." I blinked back tears as Megan's laughter once again invaded my thoughts.

"What was she like?"

"Stubborn," I replied instantly. "And sweet, adorable, funny. Loved to perform. To dance. She tried to make people laugh. She drove everyone crazy with knock-knock jokes, but could only remember the punch lines. Just a baby. She wasn't even three."

"Wow." Ashley hugged Frog. "Not even three?"

I nodded. "I wonder if she would have grown up to be a comedian. Her twin brother, Martin, was always so serious. And quite the tattle-tale. He probably would have made a good cop."

Silence and tears stretched between us, as we remembered those we'd loved and lost.

"He was right." Ashley took a deep breath. "I did leave the safe and go home. I heard the shots, and when I ran into the room he grabbed me and threw me over his shoulder. I kicked and punched him, but he wouldn't put me down. He shoved a shirt in my mouth and carried me back to the safe. Then he changed the code on the lock so I couldn't get out anymore."

I brushed back a hair from her face.

"I couldn't get out ... couldn't get back to them. Didn't even get to say goodbye." She hiccupped, reminding me of her young age.

"Ashley, how old are you?"

She stared at me, and wiped her sleeve across her nose. "Twelve and a half."

We unrolled our sleeping bags and huddled close.

Ashley turned to face me with Frog tucked securely under her arm. "What really happened?"

"Hm? What do you mean?"

"Well, one day I was in school and the next I was in the safe. All Mom and Dad would tell me was that people were angry and we had to lock ourselves away from them."

"Well," I pondered how much of recent events were okay to reveal to a twelve year old. "About four months ago, our country ran out of money."

Her brow furrowed. "How does a whole country run out of money?"

"The government gets money from taxes. And they spend money on programs, employees, military, defense and all sorts of things. For a long time they've been spending more money than the taxes have been bringing in. So we've had to borrow enough to make up the difference."

She nodded.

"I'm not sure what changed. I don't know if our lenders cut us off, or if we upset someone. All I know is that on the first of March the government stopped putting money into people's accounts. Grocery stores were full of confused and angry customers who had nothing but empty benefit cards to fill their family's growling stomachs with."

"No one had any money?" she asked.

"Some did," I replied. "But we had become way too dependent on Uncle Sam. Lots of people were on unemployment, social security or welfare. And look at how many people the government employs."

"Like teachers?" She looked thoughtful.

"Yep." I nodded. "And postal workers, politicians, IRS employees, the FBI, police, road construction crews, surveyors, military, and so many more."

"Wow." She rolled over on her back and stared at the sky. "That's like as many as the stars."

"Yeah." I nodded. "And that's a lot of people to be really upset when their paychecks weren't deposited. Tens of thousands showed up at the capitol building and fought their way inside; looking for answers."

She turned back toward me and raised herself up on one elbow. "Did they find answers?"

I sighed. "No. The building was empty. The senators had abandoned us."

"But—" Her brow furrowed. "That was only a few months ago."

"Yeah. But the nation was already in trouble. Too many had been out of work for too long. My own unemployment was about to run out. People were starving before this even happened. They kept telling us the worst of it was over. That the recession was ending. We never saw it coming."

I had always respected our laws and the authority of our country's leaders. Raised in church, I'd memorized

Hebrews 13:25 as a child. *"Obey your leaders and submit to their authority. They keep watch over you as men who must give an account."* I will not envy our leaders when they are called to give an account to their Creator as to why they forsook the people whose lives He had entrusted them to lead.

I shook my head, in an effort to eradicate such condemnatory thoughts. My mother's voice sounded in my head, reminding me that I was in no position to throw stones. "Judge not, lest ye be judged."

My own judgment day already loomed before me like an oncoming storm, growing in power and menace as it drifted ever closer. I could only pray God's grace was greater than my sins.

***April 3

THUD

The faint sound pulled me from my sleep. I grabbed my dagger from the nightstand and held my breath, waiting for confirmation that something was amiss.

Minutes passed, and nothing could be heard over the pounding of my heart. I stared at my bedroom doorway, but no boogeyman appeared.

'Just a dream, dummy,' I crept out of bed and into the living room.

But it hadn't been a dream—there was someone in my apartment. I stared at the slightly ajar door that led to the common hallway. My sanctuary had been breached.

Before I even had time to properly freak out about the situation, hard, cold metal pressed against my temple. I closed my eyes and silently prayed for an intervention.

"Hello Beautiful. Drop the knife."

I recognized the voice. It belonged to my neighbor Rodney. I had never bothered to learn his last name. I was a workaholic, and the people in my building were little more than strangers. I only knew Rodney's first name because he'd asked me out on numerous occasions, and I'd always declined.

I slowly lowered my dagger to the floor. "What do you want?"

"I was worried about you, Babe." With his spare hand he played with one of my curls.

"How thoughtful." I shuffled my feet nervously. "So you decided to ... what? Put a gun to my head?"

It took him entirely too long to ponder my question, but he'd never seemed overly intelligent. Then again, men who lean out their apartment window yelling things like 'Hot momma, shake it for daddy,' rarely are.

Rodney was carney-caliber creepy. The type of guy people would swear they saw on 'America's Most Wanted,' or one of those registered sex offender flyers. Dishwater-brown hair brushed his shoulders in a mullet, framing a gaunt face not even a mother could love. His whiskey colored eyes constantly seemed unfocused. His cologne was always the same; eau de' cheap booze and cigarettes.

He was currently sporting a shirt that boldly advertised Pabst Blue Ribbon beer.

Absolutely charming.

"I had to make sure you weren't dangerous." He stepped forward and picked up my knife. After he examined it, he slid it into the back of his jeans.

"Right, because I'm the one who broke into your apartment." I gritted my teeth.

He laughed and held up a key. "I didn't break in, I had this."

"Where did you get that?" I stared at the key he held up as my stomach filled with led.

"I asked that old wind-bag all nice-like and she just handed it over to me."

By 'old wind-bag' I assumed he was talking about the landlady—Mrs. Triton. She was a sweet little lady in her early sixties that made wonderful hot chocolate. I closed my eyes and remembered how she'd looked the last time I'd seen her.

Dread worked its way up my spine. "Please don't tell me you did something to Ms. Triton."

Rodney didn't answer. Instead, he got defensive. "You wouldn't be so uptight if you just got laid once in a while."

I was planning a real zinger of a reply when something bizarre happened. My body went on autopilot in answer to the call.

'**Duck, knee, hit, kick, grab, aim, pull.**'

My limbs responded on their own, and suddenly I was standing over Rodney with his smoking gun in my trembling hands.

So I did what any brave, in control woman would do ...

***June 14

My eyes popped open just in time to aim away from Ashley as I retched until my stomach muscles were sore. The dream ended just like it always did—with me in exactly the same fetal position I ended up in after I killed Rodney. Tears streamed down my face, as the contents of my stomach lay beside me on the ground.

Rodney had been my first kill.

I begged to forget, but I never could.

I remembered everything.

The first month, it was too risky to leave my apartment for any reason. I ate what I had in the house, rationing out my meals. After I shot Rodney I threw everything I couldn't live without into my 20 year old Honda Civic. Abandoning my apartment in Vancouver, I drove north on Highway 30, away from civilization. When my fuel light came on, I took a gravel side street and found a safe spot to park.

Mother Nature welcomed me to her bosom for the better part of two months, as I lived off the land and slept in my car. It was lonely, but I never felt completely alone in the woods.

I stayed until I felt the *call* tell me to leave again.

I've never had any delusions about my mental and physical capabilities. Only flesh and blood; fallible and mortal. These *calls*, they were not from me. Something more led me, warned me, and kept me sane. So when He tugged on me to go north, I went, concluding that the *call* was leading me to Canada, where I could find sanctuary and my best friend, Michelle.

9: Tempers

Connor

I awoke before the girls and went for a jog, not wanting to be there when they got up. Last night had changed things between the three of us, and I wasn't anxious to see the results—couldn't handle seeing pity in Liberty's eyes when she looked at me.

At least Ashley's not ignoring me anymore.

She'd graduated to scowling, but she'd finally heard me out. In less than a week Liberty had accomplished what I had been attempting for two months. I was thankful, but somewhat annoyed by her success.

A layer of dew covered the ground and my shoes were not waterproof. I could feel the mild dampness on the tips of my toes, cooling me as I ran. The morning felt crisp and clean; fresh and pure. A more optimistic man would use some cliché metaphor about a new beginning, but I was not that man. So instead of trying to compare my life to a Hallmark card, I relaxed and enjoyed the beauty.

I circled around and stayed to the south of the girls as they crossed the highway, railroad tracks, and made it to White River before noon. Looking around, I remembered why I would always call the state of Washington home. The section of the river we'd come to was nestled between two small hills packed with evergreens. Mount Rainier to the southeast and the Cascades to the east shaped a breathtaking skyline. The cool, glacier water flowed beside me, enchanting the air with its melodies.

I took a deep breath, intending to savor the moment, and smelled smoke coming from the direction that the girls were in. I shook my head and went to investigate.

They had a fire going. By the time I reached them, Liberty was holding the pan over flames while Ashley poured the white, gooey contents of a plastic bag into it.

"Seriously?" Ashley asked as she tilted the baggie up. "We're having pancakes?"

What does she think she's doing?

My fists clenched as I approached.

"Good morning Sunshine." Liberty said with a Cheshire grin.

I glowered. This was stupid. "Hey, Déjà vu. The only thing we're missing is your creepy boyfriend. Did he miss the cue?"

Her smile only widened. "He couldn't make today's performance." She jiggled the handle of the pan. "Care to take his place?"

I stood beside her, so I didn't *have to* yell, but it seemed like the only way to get through to her. "Just giving you a friendly reminder of what happened the last time you made a fire. So ... suicidal or stupid?"

Her smile turned into a teeth-bearing snarl and her eyes flashed a warning as they narrowed. She gripped the handle of the frying pan, and I took a step back, just to be safe.

"Ash, take this." She passed the handle over to the girl and shuffled through her pack, pulling out a large spoon. "Oh my." She flipped the pancake. "What on earth would I do without The Incredible Connor Dunstan to take care of me?"

Ashley giggled.

I ground my teeth. "This is foolish. Your immaturity is a danger to us all."

"How dare you! I have been watching my own back now for the full twelve years of my adult life. I don't need your protection, I don't need your manipulation, and I don't *need* you."

I blinked.

Multiple personalities? Bipolar?

She calmly removed the pancake from the frying pan, placed it on a cleaned, flat rock, and dumped more batter into the pan. The cakes were a little thin, but the fragrance was incredible. My stomach rumbled, but luckily Liberty was too busy growling to notice.

When did I last have pancakes?

"You are not in command of this expedition. I will *not* take orders from you, and you do *not have* the right to pull my strings, Geppetto." She was in my face, with her index finger pointed at my chest. "We are always in peril. We hide in shadows, sleep in bushes, and are on the move constantly. Should we give up everything that makes us happy in order to survive? If that's your idea of survival, I don't want it. I'd rather be happily dead."

She went back to preparing the food. "Right now, the promise of pancakes makes me pretty happy."

I stared at her. The risk of discovery and death seemed like a hefty price to pay for a meal. But Ashley and I had never starved; our supplies had held out. I didn't know what Liberty had been through over the last few months, but I doubted that she'd been as well provisioned as we had.

"You could have been killed." I looked her over. There was no way she could have held off that man if he'd attacked her. "Or worse."

"I had a plan and I was taking care of it!" Her voice was one decibel shy of yelling. "Did you not see the skillet to the head?" She took a deep breath, but it didn't stop her temper from coloring her face. "I've taken care of men like that before."

I chuckled and this time let my eyes drift and linger on her chest. "Oh, I bet you have."

Wonder if I can get her angry enough to self-destruct?

Her arms started to cross in front of her, but she stopped herself; clenching her fists and lowering them to her sides. "First off, *that* is none of your business. Secondly, if you think I would have allowed that shaggy, putrid, revolting excuse for a human being to have his way with me, you know *nothing* about me! I would have put my knee through his genitals or died trying."

The corner of my mouth twitched. Unsure of the exact moment my anger turned to amusement, it was an effort to keep myself from bursting with laughter. She was exactly the type of person I enjoyed getting on the stand; just blow a little smoke in her direction and she goes up like bomb fire.

"If you didn't trust me to keep Ashley safe, you shouldn't have manipulated me into taking her."

My eyebrows rose.

Hm. More like a smart bomb.

"And what should I have done?" I glanced at Ashley. "She needed to get out of there, and she wouldn't have willingly come with me."

Liberty raised an eyebrow at me. "So you left her locked in a safe with a perfect stranger, and now you're getting on my case because 'I' am putting her life in danger?"

"Let me get this straight." I tapped a finger to my chin thoughtfully. "You're screeching at me because I trusted you with Ashley?

"Screeching?" Her voice raised another octave.

"You can be as self-righteous as you want, but I did the right thing! I knew what I was doing, and I can't believe you're really arguing with me about this. You're so determined not to trust me, that you can't possibly accept that I trusted you."

She sighed, and a vast amount of anger seemed to escape with her breath. "You could have asked, you know."

"Right." I snickered. "Before or after you threatened to rename me 'Stubby'?"

"You ... you ... are so infuriating." She sounded more frustrated and confused than angry.

"I will not ever apologize for doing what I felt was right for Ashley. Don't ask me to."

After the pancake batter was depleted, Liberty dumped maple flavor into the pan. Then she added water and sugar, and stirred the mixture while it heated. Eventually the contents of the pan thickened into a runny maple syrup.

We smothered the fire, dipped the pancakes in the syrupy pan, and devoured them.

I closed my eyes and enjoyed the heavenly flavor.

After we were done eating, Ashley slipped behind a tree and left Liberty and I alone. Our anger had dissipated, but our stubbornness knew no bounds. Too intelligent to believe ourselves blameless, we were also too obstinate to concede.

She took the pan and spoon to the water and washed them, throwing occasional glances over her shoulder at me.

I decided to try again. "The pancakes were delicious. Thanks."

Her brow furrowed as she approached me, appearing to be deep in thought.

She cleared her throat. "Right now you have a clean slate, but if we're gonna do this, you have to be honest with me. We work together, or not at all. Do not lie to me and don't you dare manipulate me again."

I coughed, choking on the surprise.

So ... unpredictable.

I stared at her, baffled. Just ten minutes ago she was screaming at me.

Ground rules for a partnership?

She held out her hand. "Deal?"

10: Shelter

Liberty

Connor stared at my open hand while I wondered what was going through his mind. His expression shifted. The indifferent face of an attorney stared at me for a moment. Then the sides of his lips turned up into a grin that made me feel like guppy swimming dangerously close to a shark. But it was too late to recall the offer.

"Deal." He grasped my hand and firmly shook it.

Not to be outdone, I squeezed his hand as hard as I could.

He chuckled.

I pulled my hand away and resisted the urge to wipe it on my pants.

We headed north again, and this time Connor accompanied us. The river led us for four more days. Often we'd stop early to fish, taking advantage of the proximity of the water. The abundant catches were a blessing, and we rarely had to dip into our meager provisions.

By the time the sun reached its zenith on the fifth day, it was hidden behind angry, dark clouds. Lightning lit up the sky, accompanied by the foreboding background music of thunder. The temperature dropped quickly as the clouds split open and dumped their contents on our heads in a sudden downpour.

Connor and I each grabbed one of Ashley's hands and ran for cover toward the nearest group of trees. We huddled together and searched the area for shelter. Multiple dark houses lined both sides of our new discovery:

a golf course. We set our sights on the closest house and ran for it.

The windows were busted, but ironically, the front door was locked. Connor slipped through the broken window and let us in. The home smelled faintly of mold and dust, but that was all. Ashley and I dripped on the hardwood floor while Connor drew his knife, motioned for us to stay put, and disappeared.

The house was impressive. Vaulted ceilings, professionally painted and textured walls, classy light fixtures, and a gorgeous, brick fireplace were just a few of the features that made it so appealing. Our shoes crunched on the shattered glass from the window as we admired the custom moldings of the living room.

Ashley's teeth started chattering.

"Come on. You need to get out of those wet clothes." I grabbed her hand and headed for the stairs, almost running into Connor.

"Upstairs is clear." He scooted around us.

"Oh Ash, he's like our own, personal guard dog."

Ashley giggled as I towed her up the stairs.

Both the smaller bedrooms had belonged to boys, but the resident of the farthest room had been about Ashley's size. She grabbed sweatpants and a sweatshirt while I searched the top drawers for socks.

"Here you go." I held up a pair of the boy's underwear.

She scrunched up her face. "I don't think so."

I attempted to hand them to her, but she backed away. "Afraid they might bite you?" I giggled.

"Very funny. I don't need underclothes that bad."

I was not nearly as picky. In fact, the discovery of a clean sports bra in the master bedroom threw me into a victory dance. Finding pants was a bit trickier. My jeans used to be size twelve. I'd worked out religiously and made every attempt to diet, but try as I might; there was no squeezing my ample derrière into anything smaller. I skeptically eyed the size nine jeans that I pulled out of the dresser.

Maybe if I don't breathe.

I slid them over my legs and rear, ecstatic that they didn't get stuck, and zipped them up.

Wow! They fit!

Then, looking down at my legs, I deducted that the jeans' previous owner must have been at least a foot shorter than me. Sighing, I found a pair of men's sweatpants—at least six sizes too big—and tugged on the string until the fabric doubled over.

So much for thin.

We found Connor in the garage, surrounded by a dark cloud of smoke. A small barbeque was pushed against the open external door.

Ashley coughed and swatted at the smoke with her hand.

"We haven't even been here an hour and you're already trying to burn it down? What is it with boys and fire?" I smirked.

"Hah. Very funny." He lifted up the lid of the barbie, peeped inside and closed it. "Now get out of here and let me cook."

"Cook?" I plugged my nose. "It doesn't smell like food."

He chased us out with a spatula.

Temporarily banned from the garage and left to our own devices, Ashley and I raided the kitchen for pots and pans to use for collecting rainwater.

"I'm cold already. What if I freeze to death because you're making me get clean?" Ashley stacked another pot on the counter, following my lead.

I scrunched up my nose. "I hate to tell you this, but you stink. Bad."

"Hey!" She raised each arm and sniffed, wrinkling her nose. "Well, okay, but you stink too."

I smiled. "Yep. And it will feel so good to be clean."

While we waited for the pots and pans to fill, we swept up the broken glass and closed all the curtains. We then consolidated the collected rain water into one large pot and headed upstairs with it.

The master bathroom was breathtaking. A mahogany vanity with dual sinks rested atop the Tuscan-style tile flooring. In the corner sat a lavish, sunken tub.

I ran the tips of my fingers over hand-painted lilies on the backsplash behind the sinks. "I could live here. I wouldn't even need the whole house. This bathroom is all I need."

Ashley nodded. "Totally."

I closed the door behind me, catching a glimpse of the king-sized mahogany sleigh-bed. Okay I want the bed too."

Ashley pulled back the shower curtain, revealing the tub's jets. "Look Libby."

"Oh my. It's even a Jacuzzi."

We stared longingly at the tub.

"I really miss hot water." Ashley dipped her finger in the pot of rain water and her eyes widened. "I don't smell *that* bad."

I sniffed. "Yes, honey, you do." I handed her a container of body wash and pointed toward the towels.

Ashley sponged herself clean, complaining a little louder with each dip of the washcloth.

I stared at a wide variety of toiletries, longing for comforts that seemed more fantasy than reality.

Hot water, indoor plumbing, a safe place to live, three square meals a day.

Stuffed in the back of a cupboard I found a new, disposable razor.

Having legs that didn't look like they belonged to an orangutan.

Ashley's lips were turning purple so I walked over and helped her speed up the process.

"Libby?"

"Hm?" I dumped more water on her hair and massaged the soap out.

"I was so scared … of that guy at the lake." Water dribbled down her face and she reached for the towel. "I thought he was gonna kill me." She dabbed her eyes and wrapped up her hair. "You're so strong and you're not afraid of anything. I wish I was more like you."

I tapped her on the nose. "Ash, that's not true. I was terrified that something would happen to you. But my life … it's never been in my control." I handed her a bottle of lotion. "This stuff smells wonderful. You should use some."

She sniffed the open cap, dumped a large glob on her hand, and rubbed it in. "What do you mean?"

"I told you, you stink!"

She swatted at me with a dry towel. "Not that, about your life."

I took a deep breath. "Do you believe in God?"

"Yeah. We went to church." She handed me the lotion.

"Well, I believe that God is in control. My life—and death—are part of His plan, and no matter what I do, I can't change what he's planned.

She scrutinized me for a few moments. "So my parents dying ... that was part of God's plan?"

My eyes widened.

Foot in mouth!

"I don't know how to answer that." I let out a deep breath. "All I know is God has no restrictions, is contained by no name, and has limitless grace. He sees all things; all beginnings and ends. We only see a small piece of the puzzle, and without His foresight, we can't even begin to understand the whys of what He does."

It wasn't a great answer, but it was all I had. In truth, I was angry that He would allow this child's parents to be taken from her.

Forcing a smile I wrapped my arm around her shoulders. "You should go see if Connor has caught the house on fire yet while I clean up."

She scampered off, leaving me with my dark thoughts.

Why did they have to die?

Why have so many died?

Why do I have to live?

Are You still there?

There was no response, so I pulled off my sweats and began navigating through the scary jungle of leg hair.

This isn't so bad. Razor, shaving cream, a beautiful house to shelter us from this storm.

I took a deep breath, consciously choosing to focus on the good and not the bad. The razor ran over my leg, reminding me that shaving my legs was something I could do. A problem I could fix.

That's life I guess. You do what you can, and hope it's enough.

By the time I walked out of the bathroom, I smelled like a bouquet of flowers; jasmine scented lotion, gardenia deodorant, lilac foot rub. I'd forgotten how good it felt to smell like a woman.

I grabbed a bottle of sun block and carried it over to Ashley's open pack. The corner of a picture frame caught my eye. I "accidentally" nudged it with the sun block, until it tilted enough that I could make out a wedding photo in the silver frame bordered by roses. I picked it up and stared at the faces of strangers.

Must be her parents.

Her mother was stunning; blonde with blue eyes and a perfect button nose. The only feature Ashley shared with her seemed to be her stubborn jaw. Her father's hair was as dark as Ashley and Connor's, but his eyes were the blue-green color of the ocean. He was handsome in his own way, but with features that were very different from Connor's. Very different from Ashley's. I slid the picture back into her pack, and pondered genetics.

After my messy curls were neatly plaited and out of my face, I strolled downstairs to see what the others were up to. Connor had bowls on the table and was ladling some sort of soup into them.

"Mm." I leaned over my bowl and breathed in mouth-watering poultry spices. "Chicken noodle soup? Where'd this come from?"

"I found some cans of food in a locked pantry in the garage."

"Locked?" I raised an eyebrow at him.

Ashley handed us each a spoon.

Connor smirked and shrugged. "Whoever broke into the house probably did it early on and wasn't extremely desperate or smart. There are all sorts of treasures in the garage."

"Oh? Like what?" I shoved a spoonful of soup into my mouth. "Oh my, this is good. I don't even remember the last time I had chicken noodle soup."

Ashley slurped noodles.

Connor swallowed. "I cooked the soup in a pot on the barbeque. The propane tank is about half full."

"That is quite the find. What else is out there?" I asked.

"Oh you know ... garage stuff."

Ashley had slept between Connor and me ever since we'd made peace. At first she hadn't been thrilled about his proximity, but the benefit of Connor's body heat quickly outweighed her indignation. Ashley and I sunk into the pillow-top, king mattress while Connor disappeared into the bathroom.

Within moments her breathing leveled out. I sat up and pushed the loose hair back from her face, tucking it behind her ear. Her nose was peeling from a previous sunburn.

Glad I found that sun block. It will protect my child.

My child.

Ashley was my child now, regardless of blood or DNA. I couldn't imagine that even a maternal bond would cause me to love her more. In Ashley I'd found hope and companionship. She was someone to protect and love. To her, my humanity would be held accountable. I protected her with my life, and each day her presence helped restore my faith in mankind. Watching her sleep was so peaceful I started to drift off myself. At least until I heard the bathroom door open.

Connor stepped into the room and the musky smell of male body wash accompanied him. I mentally reprimanded myself for the little flutter in my chest. Even before the disaster, my love life had been severely lacking. Romantic interests were always neglected for my career, and men were never understanding about such things.

My two sisters had chosen families and houses. I became a business professional and never regretted the decision. My work was my life. I dated rarely, and long term relationships were well beyond my grasp. So it was my own lonesomeness—and definitely not Connor—which aroused my senses in response to his presence.

He sat down uncomfortably close to me on the bed, invading my personal space. The sweats I'd found made me look like a balloon. Connor worked his black sweats, and they accentuated the muscles in his legs. I was both thankful and disappointed that I couldn't see the back of him. A black muscle shirt completed his ensemble as it hugged his impressive chest in all the right places. His proximity suddenly made breathing very difficult.

Gulp.

He watched the peaceful face of his sleeping niece for a few moments before addressing me. "I never thanked you for taking her."

I smiled at Ashley. "And you don't have to. I didn't do it for you."

With the wedding photo fresh in my mind, I studied Ashley's face, comparing her to both parents. Then I looked at Connor. They shared so many features; nose, eyes, lips, even their eyebrows were the same.

"You're not really just her uncle, are you?" Once again curiosity had taken control of my mouth.

He swallowed, and looked at me like I was crazy. "What? Of course I'm her uncle. What does that mean?"

He's lying!

"Oh please. You're good, but you're not that good. I saw the picture of her parents."

He shook his head. "I don't know wha—"

"Stop. I held up my hand. "Don't lie to me."

He eyed me for a few minutes, and I stared right back, refusing to blink.

He let out a deep breath. "Jacob couldn't have kids. Cathy wanted a child, but Jacob wouldn't agree unless it was a relative." He shrugged. "I knew she was desperate when they asked me."

I raised an eyebrow at him.

"Cathy never liked me."

"Ashley said her mom was smart." I smirked.

Connor ignored the jibe. "My brother is ... was a good man. Always there for me, and he never asked anything in return. Well, until they wanted a child. I couldn't say no to him." He shook his head. "It was my one chance to help Jacob. And Ashley brought them both so much joy. I tried to talk him out of it at first, worried that he'd resent the child, since he couldn't ... since she wouldn't *truthfully* be his. But I should have known better. Jacob was the best father."

He walked over to his pack and pulled a little bronze figurine out. He studied it for a moment, and then stuck it in Ashley's bag.

"What's that?" I watched as he walked back toward the bed.

"Oh just something Ash got Jacob. I thought she might want it.

I sat there, dumbfounded. I looked down at the sleeping child. She slept on her side, facing the center of the bed, looking young and frail. "What are you going to do?"

"Do?" He shrugged. "I'll take care of her like I promised."

"No. I mean are you going to tell her?"

He glanced at Ashley. "Maybe eventually. I don't know. If you had a dad like Jacob, wouldn't you be disappointed to find out that *I* was actually your father? She's been through so much. I don't want to be responsible for any more hard knocks. She's just a kid."

I nodded. "I understand." My hand reached for his in an attempt to comfort him. His skin was still damp and he smelled oh so good.

He looked at my hand, then his eyes traveled up my arm and lingered a little too long on my chest.

I removed my hand and crossed my arms.

He smiled. "You helped us you know. She hated me so much, but you forced us to talk. She wouldn't even hear me out until you came along. Thanks."

I returned his smile; surprised by his gratitude. "You can thank me by being honest with her. She deserves to know."

"Bu—"

"No. You're wrong. She's stronger than you think. And who says *you* get to decide which truths people hear? I realize that your experience with the truth is lacking, since it can be quite elusive in courtrooms. But truth is not a thing to be twisted or manipulated at your will and for your benefit. It's the truth, and *your daughter* has a right to it."

Connor leaned back like I'd slapped him. Then his intense, dark eyes locked on mine. "You're not like anyone I've ever met." The corners of his mouth twitched.

"Considering that you frequent court rooms and date plastic women, I'll take that as a compliment."

"Touché."

11: Breakdown

Liberty

***March 1

I stared into the empty ice cream container, willing it to refill itself. I didn't remember eating the whole half-gallon last night, but the details preceding my sugar-induced coma were still a bit sketchy.

I eyed my furry roommate—the only other possible suspect. "Did you eat my ice cream, Kiana?"

My dog rolled over and waited for me to scratch her belly, in a surefire admission of guilt.

"Uh-huh." I scratched her belly with the toe of my slipper. "Someone is getting a little chunky."

My own bulging belly caught my eye. I'd been out of work for months, and last night's ice cream overindulgence was only the latest of my depression related binges. If I didn't find a job soon, I'd need a forklift to get me off the sofa.

"That's it, fatty. Tomorrow we're going on a diet." The name "fatty" was universal, referring to my dog as accurately us myself. Kiana closed her eyes and ignored the insult.

Wrapped in my fuzzy, blue bathrobe and slippers, with my curls sticking out in every direction, and my horrendous morning breath, I struggled to understand why no man had scooped me up yet. As I glanced in the mirror hanging above my couch, I noticed that my excessive junk food consumption was also causing a massive pimple invasion.

Depression is not my color.

I sunk into my favorite spot on the couch, ripped open the ice cream container and started licking it clean. "Ugh. What am I doing?"

Kiana raised her head and stared at me.

"Okay, that's it. We start the diet today."

Kiana rolled her eyes and went back to playing dead.

The container was tossed into the garbage in an effort to derail the temptation train. I slid back onto the couch and waited for the coffee pot to finish. A tap of the remote control snapped my thirty-six inch television to life.

"Sexual harassment, automobile accidents, wrongful death cases, if you've been wronged, we can help." I rolled my eyes at the image of Connor Dunstan promoting his law firm. "That guy is slimy with a capital S." I changed the channel.

Since the cable had been turned off, my options were limited to Daily News on NBS, Sunrise with CBA or Sesame Street on PBP. I'd had about all the disheartening reality I could handle, so I decided to spend my morning with the Muppets in their imaginary world.

The Count was just about to help Oscar the Grouch tally piles of trash when a special bulletin interrupted my morning entertainment. I flipped through the channels to avoid it, but the report monopolized all three stations. Options removed, I decided to see what all the fuss was about.

"And what did you say brought this on?" The female reporter stared into the screen, looking concerned.

The camera switched to a man who the bottom of the screen labeled as "Neil Hovich: Live at Washington DC". Background noises of crying, screaming, and confusion drowned out the man's voice. He wrapped his hands around the mouthpiece, trying to muffle the surrounding chaos, and started speaking again. But my eyes and ears had deemed him unimportant. All I could see was the grisly scene behind him, and all I could hear was terror. Riot police and Soldiers used firearms and tear gas in an attempt to control the situation. Americans killed Americans in a gas and smoke clouded scene in front of the vague outline of the Capitol building.

More meaningless words came over my speaker, and then the screen switched to "live footage" in Los Angeles, New York, Phoenix, Las Vegas, Denver and Atlanta. Death everywhere. Riots. Fires, weapons, smoke.

Bodies.

I stared; unblinking. It had to be a mistake. This couldn't be real. Not my country. Not my people. No.

My television went black and the lights went out.

The coffee machine stopped.

The horrifying sounds that had been coming from my television were now live in Vancouver, Washington.

The nightmare was real and it was just outside my door ...

***June 15

When I awoke, my heart was raw. I'd been healing, but the memory felt like it ripped the scab off prematurely. The nightmare had exhausted me, leaving my eyes gooey, and my head pounding.

I missed my dog. Memories of her battered the walls of my mind. She had hated baths, but I bathed her once a week so she would smell like expensive dog shampoo. Taking her life was the hardest decision I ever had to make. Nothing or no one else that I'd killed had been so innocent. So trusting. Her big, dark eyes stared up at me as I ran the blade—

No. Don't do this. Do not give in.

I took a deep breath, pushed back the tears, and stood up, refusing to be sucked into the black hole of despair. Ashley and Connor were not in the room, but I could hear sounds coming from downstairs.

Get dressed and join them. That'll help.

The top of the dresser was crowded with pictures. Smiling faces surrounded by a wide variety of frames watched me as I approached. Happiness. My eyes kept drifting to the wedding photo in the center. The bride's strapless wedding dress hugged her curves, and the tiara she wore made her look like royalty. Blonde hair, blue eyes, tan, beautiful.

In the picture next to it, her family knelt before a lit-up Christmas tree. Big, toothy grins surrounded by presents. I glanced at the other photos: vacation, camping trips, Disneyland keepsakes. My eyes once again sought the bride.

Gone, but where?

It was suddenly hard to breathe around the lump in my throat.

Stop staring at me!

My hands shook as I quickly laid each picture face down. I grabbed a flashlight, slipped into the walk-in closet, and closed the door behind me. I wound the flashlight, renewing its charge, and then clicked it on. The light revealed a variety of colorful clothes. Taking deep breaths, I ran my hand down the row, feeling each fabric between my fingers.

Soft, silky, smooth. Calm.

Then I saw it: the perfect little black dress; complete with spaghetti straps and a slimmer-waist.

"Grandma used to say nothing chases away the blues better than a new outfit."

I lowered the flashlight to the ground, shed my clothes, and pulled the dress over my head, wiggling as it slid over my hips. The fit was perfect. I spun around, feeling the fabric flare with the movement. The light reflected off a full length mirror on the back wall of the closet, so I stepped in front of it.

The beam shone on my lanky legs. I stared in disbelief at how much meat they'd lost. I'd always been active, sporting muscular, well shaped legs. I frowned at the shapeless sticks, and picked up the flashlight, raising the beam to my midsection. Turning to the side, I searched for the body part that had always been the bane of my exercise routine: my bottom. It was missing in action, and had left behind something too small to be natural. I patted my flat stomach.

Hm. Not all bad.

Another semi-circle turn highlighted my deflated chest.

"He was right. I *am* nothing but skin and bones."

Just one good ice cream binge and it'll all come back.

I took a deep breath and slowly raised the flashlight.

In the light's glow, my normally auburn curls appeared strawberry-blonde and frizzy. I paused, staring into my face.

No. Not my face.

My breath caught and I dropped the flashlight as I was confronted by the face of the bride in the photos.

My hands muffled a scream as the flashlight tumbled, creating an eerie strobe-light effect as her face stared back at me. A combination of guilt and fear caused my body to tremble. My knees gave way, and I landed hard on my bottom. The flashlight landed facing the mirror. The woman was gone, and my own image watched me. My eyes were sunken and haunted, surrounded by dark circles. The bones in my face, arms and shoulders protruded. Gaunt, like a walking corpse.

Why fight it? I'm so tired of fighting to survive. And for this? Is this what survival looks like?

I felt my composed façade slip away; exposing all the fears I'd tried so desperately to conceal.

Can't do this anymore.

The desire to curl up in a ball and die was overwhelming. Misery flooded the very essence of my being as I was attacked; spiritually, emotionally and mentally. I struggled for each breath; asphyxiating. Gasping until loud, wretched sobs ripped through my body. The mental walls I'd labored so hard to build crumbled at the feet of madness.

I glared at the twenty-nine year old zombie in the mirror, furious at the defeated look in my eyes. Feeling the weight of all my inadequacies, I prayed that God would end my life.

The closet door burst open. I knew it was Connor and Ashley, but didn't turn around. I wanted no witnesses when I hit the big, red self-destruct button.

Leave me alone. Let me die.

My tears turned to manic laughter as I felt their eyes burrowing into the back of my head. I glanced at the mirror and saw their worried expressions behind me.

No. Don't worry. Just leave me to die.

Kneeling on the floor, between sobs, hiccups, and frantic laughter, I opened my mouth, and grieved for all the things I'd lost.

"I miss ... my black dresses." I sniffed. "And my ... heels." I picked up a black pump from the floor of the closet; smooth and sleek. "And my sister ... oh God she's dead! Her whole family ... dead. And I think ... they did it ... themselves. She gave up! And it's so unfair that she gets to give up and I can't!"

"I've ... killed people. I didn't want ... but I had to. I had ... to, dammit." My fingers traced the lines of the black, leather pump in my hand. "Do you think God ... do you think ... he'd intervene ... had I not defended myself? Because he didn't! Where was God when I was holding that ... gun? I can't ... hear Him anymore. I want to die ... but I don't want to go to hell." My shoulders shook as tears ran down my face.

No control.

When I looked back into the mirror, Ashley was gone. Connor leaned against the closet door looking very nervous as I tried to steady my resolve. The worries and fears I'd suppressed so long became chisels, chipping away at my sanity.

What if we get to Canada and it's just as bad there?

What if my mom and Jen are dead?

How can I escape to Canada's safety when I don't even know if they're alive or dead?

Will I ever see them again?

Am I losing my mind?

What if I am not strong enough to protect Ashley?

Can I really trust Connor?

Can I trust myself with Connor?

I watched in the mirror as Connor crept forward, like he was approaching a feral animal; hands up, palms facing outward, no sudden movements. He moved in warily, and sat down Indian style beside me. His apprehensive stare formed deep lines in his forehead.

Have I baffled the Amazing Connor Dunstan?

My laughter increased and his expression darkened. A glance in the mirror justified his concern. I appeared to be deranged, displaying red, puffy eyes and blotchy skin, as an abundance of snot ran down my face.

The very definition of sexy.

I grabbed the shirt I had removed to try on the dress, and wiped away the dripping mess. "Just leave me alone. I don't want to care about you."

Feeling detached, like a spectator witnessing a fatal car crash, I stared at my reflection. Captivated by the horrific sight, I couldn't look away. Anger battled sorrow and became my predominant emotion as I scowled at the offensive mirror. This was the cause of my meltdown. Enraged, I did what any woman would do to an obviously possessed and hostile mirror: I attacked it.

Connor watched as I lunged at the mirror. My fists shattered the glass, and the pain cleared my head, pushing out unnecessary emotions that would compete with my body's warning. Shards of the mirror tumbled around me, blending their delicate symphony with my roar of fury. Connor grabbed me around the waist as I made one final blow.

Life is joy, lov,e and peace. None of which are possible without pain.

Connor scooped me up onto his lap, as blood flowed freely from the multiple slices in my hands. He took off his shirt, shredded it, and wrapped the strips tightly around my hands. Once I had been doctored to his approval, his embrace hid me from the world.

Bad idea.

The thought floated through my head for an instant, but was quickly squashed by Connor's warm, strong physique. Only a thin undershirt separated my face from his skin as I leaned into the clean, male scent of him and allowed his essence to assault my melancholy. As the flashlight began to dim, I closed my eyes and breathed him in, remembering why I fought the madness.

Every moment, each breath is a gift.

My body relaxed to the consistency of gelatin as the delirium slipped away. Dark thoughts were once again trapped behind the locked door in my mind. The heaving of my chest calmed, as my eyes sealed themselves closed.

"The conservatory is next to the ballroom," I whispered, finally remembering the layout of the *Clue* board.

"What?" Connor pushed the hair back from my eyes.

"Nothing." I hadn't meant to say it out loud. I focused once again on the game board and imagined my sisters laughing around the table. My mom yelling, as she caught us peeking at her cards.

Every memory is a blessing.

I focused on the beat of Connor's heart as the hiccups faded and my pulse returned to normal.

"I'm okay." I adjusted myself in his arms.

"Hush, I'm here, I'll take care of you."

"Egotistical jerk."

I felt the corners of my mouth twitch involuntarily before I slipped peacefully into oblivion.

12: Remembrances

Connor

***Fort Lewis, Washington, June 15

Three Generals dressed in white uniforms surrounded a large table, scrutinizing a Latino Commander. The Commander sat proudly, with his chest out and his head up.

"We've lost contact with the second team," the black-haired General said as he shifted in his chair.

The General in the center scratched his crooked nose and eyed the Commander. "We cannot afford to lose another team."

The third crossed his hands and leaned forward, staring at the second speaker. "The Progression must be stopped. The longer we wait, the stronger they become."

The Commander sat quietly as the three men discussed his fate.

The black-haired General let out a breath. "I'm afraid you're right." His mouth pursed as he considered the Commander. "Are we all in agreement then?"

"Our options are limited." The crooked-nosed General replied.

The third General leaned back in his chair and glanced at the other two who each nodded. "Commander Ortega, have your men ready to leave at oh-five hundred."

"Yessir." The Commander stood. "Just my team, sir?"

The three Generals glanced at each other.

"We need this to succeed, but we cannot continue to throw men away." The crooked-nosed General stood to his feet. "Your team plus one other. Your choice."

Commander Ortega nodded. "Commander Koyama has a solid team."

The three Generals nodded.

"Go then." The black haired General stood and offered the Commander his hand. "And may God be with you."

***

Liberty trembled in my arms. Her head rested against my chest, and with each sob, floral scented curls tickled my chin. I held still, not wanting to disturb the moment; afraid she'd pull away if she was reminded of my presence. I ignored the tickle and concentrated on the way her body melded to mine; aware of how each curve and angle fit perfectly against me.

Her breathing regulated and her shoulders loosened as she surrendered to sleep. I gently moved out from under her, picked her up, and carried her to the bed. She stirred as I laid her down. Soft skin met thin eyebrows under my fingertips, as I brushed the hair out of her face. Sitting beside her with my back against the headboard, I rested my eyes and listened to her breathing.

****A small village in the Safid Mountain Range, Afghanistan, eight years ago*

It was completely dark when we came upon the small village hidden in a lower slope of the Safēd Kōh. My team of six was here to rendezvous with an informant, exchanging currency for information on the whereabouts of a group of terrorists.

The five sergeants with me made up half of my ODA Special Forces team. Each chosen for their abilities, they were intelligent, deadly, and completely trustworthy.

Michael Winters was an almost seven foot tall black man who could build—or destroy—anything. He grew up in Boston, the fourth child of six. His parents were both still alive and had just celebrated their fortieth wedding anniversary. I only knew of this because the event was so important to Winters he had taken leave for it.

Phillip LeFord was quite possibly the thinnest man I'd ever met, despite an appetite that could put any all-you-can-eat buffet out of business. From a small town in Wisconsin, he was a dedicated cheese head. During football season, he always managed to follow his Packers—no matter where we were and what we were doing. His job was to keep us in constant communication with the other six members of our team who were currently in the air.

Terrance Vaughn, at a little over five-foot-five with blonde hair and a scar over his left eyebrow, was our medic. He was the newest member of the team, joining about six months ago. He was young and incredibly gifted. The men called him Doogie after Doogie Howser, the boy-genius doctor.

Rick Bilford was the oldest member of the team at thirty-four, and acted as team daddy. Commander was my title, but Rick was the old man who kept us all in line. He grew up on a ranch in Texas, and was the very definition of a good 'ole boy; chivalrous, religious, and stubborn as a mule.

Completing the team was Carlos (Boom) Ortega—a walking oxymoron as our devout Catholic weapons specialist. We called him Boom because destruction was his middle name. He liked big explosions and always created the best distractions. He was the only other Washington state native on our team, and had become like a brother to me. There was no man I'd rather have at my back.

The operation was standard. Get in, get the info, pay the man, and get out. The bag I carried held $251,000 afghanis; which equaled about $5,000 US dollars. The meeting point was just inside the villa; easy to find with the aid of night-vision goggles. Third door from the entrance in the wall, in through the back door, wait for the contact. We spread out and huddled against the walls, covered by the shadows of the building.

The exchange was to happen at 02:00. My watch read 01:45 when someone entered through the north door. My night-vision revealed a child, under ten, thin and trembling as he took one tentative step forward, and then another. He hesitated, searching the room, until his eyes rested on LeFord's leg which was barely visible in the light from the window. Something on the child beeped, and a light flashed on his chest. He looked down and gasped, and then headed slowly toward LeFord. His chest beeped again.

I commanded the boy to stop in the local dialect of Pashto. He paused for a moment and glanced in my direction. His chest beeped again and he took another step toward my communications man—my responsibility.

I aimed my weapon and demanded that the child stop.

No one breathed as the boy's foot slid across the floor in another step closer. His chest beeped again, and I squeezed the trigger. The three-shot burst from my semi-automatic hit him in the head, and he fell.

"No!" LeFord stood and ran to the dead boy.

"LeFord! Get over here." I whispered the words through clenched teeth.

He bent and removed the glowing light from the boy's chest. Shaking his head, he stood and raised his find into the air: a watch. "Not a bomb," he said as it beeped again.

We all let out a breath. I stared at the body—the child I just killed over a watch.

"Why—" Bilford's question was interrupted by the gunfire that ripped apart LeFord's chest. His body swayed with the force of each round before he crumbled to the floor.

The shots had come from behind us.

"He was a distraction. Everyone down!" I shouted as I crawled to LeFord's body, turning my head just as the shot that should have killed me grazed my jaw. My hand *found the wound and came away warm and wet, but it wasn't fatal. I pulled LeFord out of the light, and back to the shadows of the wall.*

"Not a bomb." Blood dribbled from his lips as he muttered the words. "Just a kid."

"Hush. It's okay." I forced myself to watch as blood rushed from LeFord's chest. "Stick around kid; you know Green Bay can't win without you."

He forced a smile.

Vaughn eyed my jaw.

"It's just a scratch. See if you can do anything for LeFord."

Vaughn kneeled and examined LeFord's chest, shook his head at me, and returned to his post by the west door, firing shots into the hall.

Boom looked from Vaughn to me, to LeFord, and then crouched and put his head next to the dying man. "The Lord is my shepherd—"

I caught pieces of the prayer he muttered between gunfire.

"—He restoreth my soul—"

Anger clouded my vision as I fired off another round at a movement outside the north door.

"Yea, though I walk through the shadow of the valley of death—"

Winters peeked out the window beside me and fired.

"Thou preparest a table before me in the presence of mine enemies."

A tear slid down my cheek as I remembered the picture of LeFord's mom that he carried in his wallet. He was an only child to a single mother. I reloaded the 30-round magazine and clipped it back onto my M-16.

"—and I will dwell in the House of the Lord forever." Boom crossed himself and stood up, handing me LeFord's dog tags. I pocketed them; his mother would want the tags.

I grabbed Winter's arm. "We need an evac."

With LeFord dead, Winters stepped into the position of communications. He held his radio before his mouth and pushed the button. "*Dark Delivery to Momma Bird, come in momma bird.*"

"*You're early Dark Delivery. What's going on down there?*" The voice on the other end was distorted by frequency static.

"*The parrot didn't fly in; we need an evac.*" Winter's words were delivered between shots as he ducked and Bilford stepped into his place in front of the window. A shot whizzed by Bilford's ear as he shuffled to the right.

In the moonlight I could see figures darting back and forth outside the doors.

"*How many? Anyone got a count?*"

"*Three or four here.*" Boom counted the figures out the south window.

"*Maybe four in the west wing.*" Vaughn threw a grenade into the hall, and ducked as shrapnel and fire filled the air. "*West looks clear.*"

"*At least eight out the north.*" Bilford took aim and fired out the window.

"*Bilford, Vaughn, Winters, out the south door. Boom, let's light up the north.*"

Boom crept to the north window and crouched beside me. A grenade appeared in his hand. He pulled the pin and threw it out the window. An enemy shout sounded, and dark figures scattered away from the path of the flying bomb. Boom and I opened fire on the running targets, taking down three. Three more disappeared during the impact of the blast.

"*Time to go,*" I whispered and turned toward the southern door.

Boom provided cover as I slipped out the door. Then the spray from my M-16 kept our enemies ducking instead of shooting as Boom followed. Once outside, he added the throw of another grenade to my rifle assault. We used the distraction of the explosion to run toward the wall where Bilford, Vaughn and Winters waited for us.

Vaughn tended to Bilford, who sat with his back against the wall. Bilford looked pale, and blood covered the ground beside him. Vaughn's hands were red and dripping as he wrapped Bilford's side, applying pressure.

"What can I do?" I kneeled next to Bilford as Boom and Winters fired off shots to enforce the perimeter.

"He's gonna be fine. Gonna make it." Vaughn didn't look sure of his own words.

Bilford's hand covered a cough and when he pulled it away, his fingers were red. "I'm dying and you know it, kid. Got me in the gut. We both know I'm not leaving this stinkin' desert." He struggled to remove his wedding ring.

"Let me help." I grabbed his hand and twisted off the ring.

He nodded. "Tell Mary-Beth I'll be waitin' for her." He coughed again, and blood sprayed his chest. "There's a pocket watch in my trunk. Was m' daddy's. Make sure little Ricky gets it."

"Of course." I swallowed but it did nothing to relieve the lump in my throat. Rick Bilford was a good man. He was supposed to retire next year—he wanted to be home for little Ricky as the boy started high school.

"Mi hermano," Boom said, grasping Bilford's hand. "Save a spot for me at the Father's table."

Bilford forced a smile. "Will do. Send me off with a bang, my friend."

Boom's lips spread into a wide smile as he felt for the remote in his pocket. He'd laid C4 along the wall on our way in.

"Momma bird, we need air support." Winters spoke the words into his radio between shots. "Copy. Ready to move."

Winters signaled and we took off running as the F-22 Raptor showed up. The popping sounds from the air meant that the jet's M61 provided us with the cover we needed. Its twenty millimeter rounds tore up the ground behind us as we sprinted away, heading for the protection the slope in front of us would afford. We jumped over the ridge as I did a quick head count.

"Boom, Vaughn, Winters." Only four left of the six. I sighed. "Light it up, Boom."

"Father, guide their souls." Boom crossed himself as he pressed the button.

*** *June 15*

I awoke with a crick in my neck from falling asleep in the awkward, sitting position. I rolled my head from shoulder to shoulder and remembered the send-off we'd created for Bilford and LeFord—two men whose lives I'd never forgive myself for losing. I ran my finger down the scar on my chin.

Knuckling my eyelids, I tried to erase the vision of the child I'd murdered. I should have recognized the distraction, should have paid more attention to what was happening outside. I was their Commander and I had let them down.

I remembered how LeFord's mom cried out in sorrow when I closed her hand around his dog tags. I'd never forget the face of little Ricky when I gave him his father's pocket watch.

I wouldn't care like that—couldn't be that vulnerable—ever again.

Faint snoring sounds came from Ashley and Liberty, grating on my nerves. I stared at them. Ashley, my brother's daughter; I'd donated the sperm, but I'd never replace Jacob. She'd never forgive me, never love me. But it didn't matter. I didn't ask for a kid, and I was sick and tired of looking after someone who wouldn't even talk to me.

Screw it, Jacob. If you care so much, you come take care of her.

Liberty looked so peaceful. I leaned forward to kiss her, and her voice echoed in my head.

"I don't want to like you."

The words she'd said earlier swirled around in my head, severing nerves, summoning anger. I scowled at Liberty's scrawny body. Kissing her would probably be like kissing frozen metal anyway. I stood up and glared at the girls.

What am I doing? I don't care about them.

Liberty rolled to her side, turning her back to me even in her sleep.

And I don't want to like you either.

13: Normal

Liberty

"Put your little foot,
Put your little foot,
Put your little foot right out."
My grandfather sang as he led me through the dance.
 "Take a little step,
Take a little step,
Take a little step right out."
He twirled me around and I giggled like the grandpa's little girl I would always be.

The room around us—if it was actually a room—was white and void of all furniture or walls. The distance was cloudy, and all I could see was right in front of me: my grandfather.

Lines creased his warm, loving face. Blue-grey eyes that always appeared amused stared down at me.

Down at me?

The last time I'd danced with my grandfather I was almost a foot taller than him. But at this moment in time, I was frail and small standing in his shadow. My hand felt insignificant surrounded by his.

I stared into the familiar eyes that seemed more than human.

"Grandpa, am I ... dead?"

He stopped suddenly, and a loving smile spread across his face. "No, my little Liberty Bell, God has plans for your life."

A tear slid down my cheek as I realized I had been hoping for a different answer.

"But I'm so tired," I complained.

He ignored the comment and led me into the next step.
"La de dumpty dah dah,
La de dumpty dah dah."
I didn't want him to leave; didn't want to be alone. I held his hand tightly and prayed that the dance would last forever.

***

When I opened my eyes, the first thing I saw was Ashley's worried face. She was biting her bottom lip and staring out the window.

I'm not alone.

She jumped when I shifted and started to sit up. My head objected to the change in elevation and vengefully made me nauseous.

"You're awake!" She cheered.

I grimaced at her loud, high pitched voice, and grunted in response.

"What's wrong? Can I get you something? Are you hungry? You weren't out for very long. Do you want to go back to sleep?"

"Stop." I held my hands up. "Please. Stop. I'm fine."

Just after effects of a minor mental breakdown.

She bit her lip and lowered her eyes at my harsh tone.

"But since you're offering—" I tried to smile; sure it looked more like a grimace. "I would like a half inch thick prime rib, a huge salad with blue cheese dressing, a chocolate cake, and a bottle of merlot."

"Uh-huh." She stared at me skeptically.

"Okay fine, you big cheapskate, I'll settle for anything off the Taco Bell Menu. Well okay, anything but the quesadillas, I never did like those much."

"You are so weird." Relief replaced worry in her eyes, as she jumped on the bed and wrapped me in a bear hug.

I tried not to throw up as her bouncing jostled my upset stomach and rattled my traumatized brain.

"You scared me. You gonna be okay?"

I took a deep breath and squeezed her back. "Yeah, kiddo, I'm fine. Everything just seemed a bit overwhelming and I needed time to deal. Understand?"

Ashley nodded, scampered off the bed, and disappeared. A few minutes later she returned with a glass of water and two aspirin.

"I've died, and you're my own personal angel, aren't you?" I teased.

She smirked and handed me the medicine, which I accepted and washed down. Ashley took the glass from me and set it on the nightstand. With no other immediate ways to attend me, she hovered and fidgeted until I got out of bed.

When I stood, I realized I was still wearing the catalyst for this morning's attack of insanity. I went to the closet and pushed open the door, expecting to find broken glass everywhere. But the hardwood floor was clean.

I looked down at my hands and confirmed that they were still wrapped in strips of Connor's shirt. I untied the cotton bandages and admired the damage I'd done to my fists. The cuts and bruises were minor; nothing that wouldn't heal.

I stepped into the closet and exchanged my black nightmare for a more casual knit dress. It was clingy and hugged my curves, but was comfortable in its stretchy mobility. I grabbed the brush off the dresser, raked it through my hair a few times, and then confronted the bathroom mirror.

I looked a mess, but nothing like the train wreck I'd been earlier. My long, curly hair was frizzy, but not frighteningly so, and the red puffiness of my eyes had been greatly reduced by the much needed sleep. It would have to do. It wasn't like I was planning on winning any beauty pageants.

When my head finally stopped pounding, we went downstairs and found Connor in the garage. He had a cabinet door open and appeared to be going over the food inside. He looked up at our approach, and then froze as his eyes locked on mine. I showed him my teeth and hoped I looked mentally stable and reassuring.

Yes, I'm fine. This nut hasn't completely cracked yet.

I stepped out of his eye-lock and into the garage to investigate. There were bikes on the rack, a lawn mower to the left, a canoe hanging up, and ...

"Holy cow, those are bikes!" I regretted the volume of my happiness when it caused my head to resume its rhythmic throbbing.

Connor nodded. "Yeah. We're gonna bike the rest of the way."

He sounded different; distracted, cold.

I looked at Ashley, and her brow furrowed.

"What's wrong Ash?"

"I haven't ridden a bike in forever. I don't know if I'll remember how." She eyed the bikes dubiously.

"They say you never forget." I reassured her. "Only one way to find out."

Ashley and I pulled the bikes off the rack and inspected them. I adjusted her seat and she wheeled it around the small, unoccupied space of the garage. The verdict was that she'd manage.

I was tempted to grab the man's bike and leave the woman's to Connor, but since he'd been surprisingly supportive during my crazy-time, I decided to play nice. I adjusted the woman's bike seat for my long legs.

Once the bikes were ready, we stood in uncomfortable silence, glancing at each other. Connor and I excelled at yelling and screaming, but civil communication had proven to be beyond our abilities. The fact that he'd seen me at my weakest left me feeling exposed and vulnerable.

Will he think I'm a liability now?

No, that's crazy. He held me—helped me.

He fidgeted and opened the grill, so I came closer to peek inside. I glimpsed a large pot before he intercepted me.

"Nope." He pulled the lid closed and blocked my view.

I feinted to the right then stepped to the left; trying to reach around him and open it, but he grabbed my wrist.

"Dammit, Liberty. You don't listen." He released my wrist and turned his back on me.

What the—?

I raised an eyebrow at Ashley. She shrugged and walked toward the door that led back to the kitchen. I followed, glancing back at Connor who seemed intent on ignoring us both.

"What's with him?" I asked, shutting the door behind me.

She shrugged. "How should I know? You're both crazy." She smiled sheepishly. "I didn't mean crazy, crazy. I mean—"

I held up my hand. "No, I get it. And you're right." I raised my right hand over my head. "You must be at least this crazy before you ride the rollercoaster of adulthood."

Ashley and I hunted through kitchen drawers and cupboards until we found linen placemats and napkins and matching dinner plates. We set the table, and then filched two small candles from a decorative display on the wall. Since the heavy winter curtains fully covered the windows, we felt safe enough to light the scented wax and add ambiance to our elegant table setting.

Connor opened the door and the palatable aroma of spaghetti encompassed him. His eyes lingered on the table. Ashley and I held our breath, presuming he would object to the candles, which would in turn lead to a long, exhausting argument.

He shook his head, moved toward the table, and set the pot of spaghetti on the hot-pad we'd placed for it.

Ashley and I cast confused glances at each other as we sat down.

The meal by candlelight seemed surreal. Like the dream of my grandfather, only the area around us was visible. We sat at a mahogany table with matching chairs. A chandelier hung just above the center of the table, refracting the light into hundreds of shapes and colors. The table was centered on a Tuscan rug that rested over the hardwood floor. It was all so beautiful—so perfect. Everything felt so ... normal.

The candlelight emphasized certain details about Connor that I tried unsuccessfully to ignore. Like the extraordinary length of his eyelashes, his perfectly shaped, masculine lips, and the way shadows danced across his strong jaw bone when he spoke; undeniably handsome.

And dangerous. Don't forget dangerous.

And glaring at me! What's his problem?

After we washed up the dinner dishes, Ashley grabbed a pot of rainwater and scampered upstairs, leaving Connor and I dangerously alone. I pushed the chairs in around the table as he put away the place settings.

I wiped down the counters for the third time before deciding I was done with the uncomfortable silence routine. I put my hands on my hips and faced him. "What's your problem?"

He chuckled and turned to stare at me. "*I* don't have a problem."

I glared back. "You know what ... forget it. Fine. No not fine. Just when I think you could possibly be a decent human being, you always have to prove me wrong."

"Oh that's rich." He leaned against the wall. "*You're* the one who doesn't want to like *me*, remember?"

I blinked.

What the—?

"Remember? I was trying to help you, and as usual you made sure to tell me how much you didn't need my help. Would it kill you to be a little appreciative?" He slammed the door to the cupboard he was searching through.

"You jerk." I threw the rag I held into the sink. "I meant that I was starting to like you, and I didn't want to." My eyes narrowed further. "Of course I can't imagine why I wouldn't want to like you. You're so *incredibly charming.*"

I walked toward the stairs and he grabbed my arm, spinning me around to face him. His warm hand reminded me of how good his arms had felt around me.

No. Must be strong.

We stood; our mulish expressions just inches from each other as the seconds ticked by. Finally I gritted my teeth, yanked my arm away from his grasp and escaped up the stairs.

"That's okay. I don't like you either!" He yelled.

"Yeah, that's real mature!" I slammed the bedroom door behind me.

14: Frustration

Connor

I clenched my fists and counted to ten as the most infuriating female I'd ever had the misfortune of knowing stormed up the stairs.

Five hours ago the complex web of Liberty was unraveling in my arms. I had seen a glimpse of the soft, scared woman who hid behind the stand-offish ice queen. And for just a moment she'd allowed me to comfort her.

"Stupid," I berated myself aloud and punched the wall. The broken plaster and bloodied knuckles did nothing to soothe my temper.

I shoved my feet into tennis shoes and laced them up. A run would clear my head and save helpless walls from my wrath. The heavy rain sounded against the roof, but real Washingtonians never let a little drizzle slow us down. I pulled on a hooded jacket and headed out the front door.

After a good stretch I started off fast—determined to run until rain and exhaustion battered my attitude into submission. Methodically, I kept putting one foot in front of the other, hoping the familiar motions would persuade my mental state to return to normal. I shook my head, trying to rattle loose whatever blocked my brain.

She always pushes me away.

Listening to my footfalls splashing in the water, I banished the sound of her voice from my head.

Nothing I say is right.

Concentrating on the clean fragrance of rain, I pushed aside thoughts of her scent.

She's not exactly perfect.

My pace increased as I tried not to dwell on how her strength and determination encouraged my own.

Everything is a challenge with that woman!

Focusing on my breathing, I struggled to understand what I felt for her.

How can one person complicate life so much?

I ran until my anger lost steam in proportion with my feet, and before long both sputtered out. I stuck to the sides of the course; hiding in the foliage. Even in the fading light, I could tell that this had been an upscale country club. Tasteful houses lined both sides of the course in an array of homeowner's association approved colors. Although the grass was long and unruly, the landscape was still commendable.

The ninth hole was a par four with a tricky water hazard, causing me to wish I had my clubs. I'd enjoyed golf once—enjoyed life completely. As a senior partner in a prosperous law firm, I had multiple prospects, a great house, two nice cars, plenty of money in the bank, stocks, and bonds. I wanted for nothing; possessed everything. Anything I required was within my grasp.

But each second since my brother's death worked to emphasize the true inadequacy of my life. All along I'd lacked the one thing I truly needed: time.

'Sorry, Jacob, I don't have time to come to dinner tonight, give my best to the wife and kid.'

'Sorry, Jacob, big client coming into town, can't make that tee time.'

'Sorry, Jacob, have to work on Thanksgiving—big case.'

Each painful memory of the numerous times I'd disappointed my brother was on some sort of torturous loop in my subconscious.

'Sorry, Jacob, I'd love to shoot hoops, but I just can't get away today.'

'*Sorry, Jacob ...*'

He was so understanding, making it easy for me to take him for granted. Jacob had been the one constant in my life. He never changed, never wavered; forever waiting for me to come around.

I was sixteen when our parents died in the car crash, and Jacob was nineteen. He'd been at college for less than a year, but didn't hesitate to take me in. He always came through.

My best friend.

And I killed him.

Jacob was the perpetual Samaritan. He was my conscience—my own, personal, Jiminy Cricket— determined to keep me on the straight and narrow. No matter how many times I slipped from the path he was always there to pull me back up. Without him, I felt incomplete; like yin without yang. The void his absence created was beyond my comprehension. The thought of never seeing my brother again was unfathomable.

I had turned Jacob into another Afghanistan casualty; effectively blocking him from my life. His eyes had held so much hurt when he confronted me about ignoring his calls.

"No, Jacob, I don't want to talk about Afghanistan," I insisted for the umpteenth time.

"Connor, don't shut me out. It wasn't your fault. You did everything you could for those men." He paced the floor of my living room.

I had been avoiding him for months, pouring myself into my law studies. My bar exam was rapidly approaching, and I hid behind that very compelling excuse. I would have left, had he warned me that he was coming over.

I closed the textbook I was studying and stared up at Jacob. "You don't know what you're talking about. Those men were *my* responsibility. They trusted *me* to be a proficient Commander."

He paused in front of me, crossing his arms. "What could you have done differently?"

"I should have known that kid wasn't carrying a bomb— shouldn't have shot him." I stood toe-to-toe with my brother. "I should have been intelligent enough to see the trap!"

"You did the best you could." He grabbed my shoulder. "You're a good man, Connor."

The image of the boy I'd shot over a watch flooded into my mind. "Am I?" I shook my head, dissipating the vision. "If I hadn't shot that kid, LeFord wouldn't have exposed himself. *I* murdered a child, and LeFord paid the price."

"You made a mistake. You can't shut the world out because of it."

But I'd proven him wrong. I passed the bar and effectively cut everyone I cared about out of my life. I became the kind a man my father would have hated—a man my brother could barely stand to look at. And he still didn't give up on me.

"This isn't you, Con, you're a good man." His words rang through my mind, conflicting with the image I'd worked so hard to fabricate.

"I miss you, bro." I wondered if he could hear me, wherever he was. "I wish you were here." My throat constricted and I couldn't say anymore. The damn rain kept pelting my eyes; blurring my vision.

I slowed to a walk as my thoughts turned back to my immediate problem: Liberty. Eight years in the army and six years as an attorney left me inadequately equipped to deal with the frustration Liberty Collins brought into my life. I never had to work at romance before. Take a woman to dinner, buy her some flowers or maybe a nice piece of jewelry, show her some attention, bathe her in compliments, and voila—romance.

Liberty was different. Full of piss and vinegar, that's what my father would say. Like a thistle, strong and beautiful, but with sharp, protective prickles. What would any sane man want with a woman like that?

What do I want with her?

I stopped, and leaned over, stretching my thigh and back muscles. My left eye twitched and I knuckled it, trying to force it to stop. The twitching continued. I widened my eyes, and then narrowed them. I pulled on the eyelid, and then pushed it in. Nothing helped.

Taking deep breaths, I mentally practiced the encouragement I'd repeated to myself before many trials.

I am a consummate professional, hiding my emotions behind a wall of indifference, projecting the calculated indifference of my position.

My eye continued to twitch.

I. Don't. Twitch.

It was amazing that one person could provoke *my* anger, confusion, frustration, and desire so powerfully, and often in the same moment. I blew out a breath.

I wasn't being fair. She wasn't always an insufferable nuisance. In one fleeting moment I'd seen her weak and vulnerable; a fragile ice sculpture melting in my arms. I could still smell her hair and skin. Not the floral fragrances she'd applied, but the underlying scent that made up the woman.

Soft, full lips tempted me to find out if she tasted as good as she smelled. Her jade colored eyes were intense and mesmerizing. Her wild, red hair mirrored her spirited nature.

Inaccessible, guarded, cold. I watched helplessly as she cracked, terrified that she'd break.

No. Can't think like that. Don't get close. She's not what you want. And she doesn't want you.

The rain mellowed to a drizzle. I sat on a bench near the side of the trail. Rain soaked my clothes, cooling me down as I remembered the day I found Liberty.

Ashley had just become a woman. At least that's what she told me when I saw the blood on the floor. Since our supplies were lacking in feminine products, I found myself searching through the cabinets of the upstairs bathroom of an abandoned house.

A scream pierced the air. I hid behind the curtain and peeked out the window. As I watched, a black hooded sweatshirt and blue jeans jogged by; tall, thin and female.

From my viewpoint I could see two people about a block behind the first, and gaining on her.

I ran downstairs and slipped out the back door. I chased after her before I consciously made the decision to do so.

What am I doing?

I crossed one yard, and then the next, hoping I'd cut her off at the following intersection. I had to get to her; to help her. By the time I caught up, there was no time for words. I grabbed the girl and carried her into the bushes to hide.

She was light, weighing in at maybe a buck twenty-five, which was unhealthy for her five-foot-nine height. When she struggled, my hands felt more bone than flesh.

How has she survived this far?

I wrestled her to the ground and lay on top of her, afraid she would break under my weight. She continued to squirm, causing friction against body parts neglected for too long. Despite the fact that we were in danger, things were about to get somewhat awkward when she bit my hand.

Within five minutes of meeting Liberty, I had my first ever thought of striking a woman. I would never follow through with it, but I'd be lying if I said the idea hadn't crossed my mind. When I stood, I had every intention of leaving her behind. A complete stranger—with sharp teeth—and I didn't know who or what she had been running from. Besides, I had Ashley to think about.

'You can't abandon her.' Jacob's voice sounded in my head.

I looked down at down at the woman who still had a death grip on her dagger as she glared at me.

She's not exactly helpless.

'Help her, Con. This is your chance. Prove that I was right about you.'

I stood and stretched again, wondering if Jacob was watching me from Heaven, enjoying my misery with a large, buttery popcorn in one hand and a root-beer in the other.

Yeah, Bro. Laugh now, but someday I'll get you back for this one.

Thoroughly soaked, I headed back toward the house. Within a few yards, the hair on the back of my neck stood up, accompanying the feeling that I was being watched. I glanced around, but noticed no movement. Chalking up the paranoia to misplaced dread of another confrontation with Miss. Congeniality, I took the long way back. Weaving through yards, I stopped often to listen for sounds of pursuit. Confident that I had been imagining things, I slid into the borrowed house and climbed the stairs.

Washed up and with dry clothes on, I stepped out of the master bathroom to find a sleeping Ashley curled up into a ball in the center of the king bed. The curtains were closed, and Liberty had a flashlight crammed into the bottom of the top dresser drawer. She was lying on the floor, on her stomach, reading a paperback under the light.

"Ashley passed out early?" I whispered.

Liberty attempted to jump out of her skin, and then glared at me. Her expression softened into a loving smile when she glanced at Ashley.

I watched her face, wishing that she'd direct a fraction of the affection she felt for Ashley toward me.

I took a deep breath.

You've seen mediators in action. You can do this.

"We should talk." I felt the tension rise as she scrutinized me for a moment, rolled over, and sat up. Her shoulders slumped and she let out a deep breath.

Did I always have this effect on women?

"Talk?" She sounded skeptical as she closed the paperback and placed it on top of the dresser. "Now you wanna talk? And they say *women* have mood swings."

"Right. Never mind." I turned to leave, but she reached out and grabbed my leg. I stopped and looked over my shoulder at her.

She cast her eyes downward. "I'm ... I'm not used to relying on anyone but myself. Needing help is—" She swallowed, suddenly looking much younger than twenty-nine. "I just ... I mean ... Thank you. I'm sorry." Her expression became a mix of emotions I couldn't begin to read.

I blinked.

Exactly how many personalities does this girl have?

She patted the floor beside her. As I sat down she studied my bloody knuckles, raising an eyebrow.

I shrugged, and her mouth twitched.

Oh yeah, she wants me.

"So … trying out the whole talking thing." I cleared my throat and turned on my best talk show host voice. "Let's start by digging into the depths of the mysterious mind of Liberty. Liberty Collins, what are you thinking about right now?"

She tapped her head. "Right this minute?"

I nodded.

"I'm regretting all the times I skipped dessert."

I chuckled and considered her.

What is it about this woman that throws me off guard?

The dress she wore accentuated her narrow waist as it flowed into the curves of her hips. Her curls were barely contained in a clip on the top of her head, and the light gently caressed her long neck. I wanted to trace the lines of her collarbone with my lips.

Natural: from her appearance to her personality, Liberty's presence was her own, uninfluenced by others, like a candle that wouldn't be snuffed out by changing winds. I held my breath as the desire to protect and possess her overcame me.

Whoa. She'd kill me if she could read my mind.

Pull yourself together!

"Connor, what do you want?" She raised one eyebrow and looked at me like I was a curiosity. "And what's up with your eye?"

Crap! Twitching again!

I rubbed the overactive eyelid and shrugged. What did I want? Good question. She looked beautiful and helpless, but I knew the truth. She was attractive, but she was autonomous. I'd once had money, power, and stability, but what did I have now to offer to a woman like Liberty? She'd already made it very clear she didn't 'need' me.

"I—I think we should talk about the plan," I replied, deciding on neutral territory. "I know we are heading north, but you haven't told me where. I should probably know."

It was a lie. I knew exactly where she was taking us. I also knew it was futile. No country on this planet had a chance of being unaffected by the failure of the US. Canada's current state would no doubt be very comparable to ours. But Liberty had a goal and hope. Who was I to take these things away from her?

"Why?" she asked.

I tilted my head, unsure of what she was asking.

"Why do you want to know?" Her face flushed in the tell-tale sign that her temper was flaring. "Are you planning on leaving me behind if I have another spell like earlier?" Ice cubes could have formed from her words.

I leaned away, watching the fire burning in her eyes. I heard her words, but they made no sense.

What is she talking about?

She stood and started pacing like a caged lion. "I had a bad day. It won't happen again. I'm better now. And if you think you can take Ashley away from me, then you're the one who's crazy."

I used the dresser to pull myself to my feet while I considered what she was saying. "Ashley is my—"

Suddenly Liberty was inches from my face. Her finger held my lips closed. Her jaw unclenched and her shoulders slumped. The anger in her eyes turned to sorrow. "Connor, please don't do this. Don't take Ash from me."

She slowly pulled her finger away from my face and hugged herself. I watched her lips move. My eyes tracked the single tear that slid down her cheek.

No. I won't hurt you. Not ever.

What could I say? How could I put my feelings into words and make her believe them? Could I kiss her?

I was leaning forward into uncertain doom when Ashley stirred. The sound pulled me from my trance and made me acutely aware of how hard my heart pounded.

Take a step back. Think about this.

Liberty resumed her pacing as I went to Ashley. In her stirring, she had kicked off the covers, so I pulled them up over her shoulders and tucked them under her chin. She smiled, obviously enjoying her dream. I pushed a loose strand of hair out of her face and thought about Liberty.

I'd almost kissed her. Would she have allowed it? Was it what she wanted? What I wanted? What I—

Liberty gasped.

I pushed away from the bed, turning toward the door. Liberty's hands were in the air and the silver chamber of a pistol rested against her head.

15: Retribution

Connor

"Oh, I'm sorry, am I interrupting something?" The man holding the gun to Liberty's head showed his teeth in a malicious grin.

He looked like he'd be much more comfortable holding a surf board and a six pack of beer than a pistol. His dark tan contrasted with chin-length sandy-blonde hair and blue eyes.

"Mark Fletcher," I replied through clenched teeth, hoping Liberty would recognize the name.

Her breath caught and her eyeballs rolled to the side, widening when she caught a glimpse of her captor.

Good. She's heard of him.

The look on his face confirmed that my fear was warranted—Fletcher had jumped off the pier of sanity into a whole ocean of crazy. His gaze darted nervously around the room as his finger twitched on the trigger.

I knew him professionally. Fletcher had been the intended successor of a large and prosperous furniture chain based out of Olympia. Fletcher Furniture had flourished for generations, passed down from first son to first son for as long as anyone could remember. But when Mark took over, his family learned that he couldn't handle the power that came with the position.

Evidence of his power abuse first surfaced about two years ago when a pretty, little blonde doll stepped into my office under the watchful gaze of her father. According to the young lady, Fletcher had promised her a position in the business, if she could first prove her skill at numerous positions in his bedroom.

After their clothing-prohibited interview, he voiced his disappointment in the girl's performance, and invited her to bring a friend and try again. Instead she went to her father, who was more than a little offended by Mark's pre-employment screening practices, and hired me to go after him.

I went digging and found multiple victims who'd experienced their own harassment nightmares from the depraved heir to the furniture fortune. Evidence was sound, and once they realized the financial potential of their misadventures, victims were more than willing to come forward. The system demanded justice, and all offended women were awarded healthy recompense.

Daddy Fletcher, fearing for the reputation of the family business, promoted his second son to successor and wrote Mark Fletcher out of the family business plan. The media feasted on the drama, and store profits grew due to the shrewd morals of the father.

The victory had tasted exquisite, as adrenaline pumped through my veins when the courtroom erupted in cheers. The villain was convicted and punished for his crimes.

Now the villain held a gun to Liberty's head.

I'll kill him this time.

"What's the matter?" The flashlight cast shadows on Mark's face, highlighting his sunken eyes. "Not so tough without a bailiff between us?" He shifted his feet. "You have nothing to say to the man whose life you ruined?"

"Why are you here?" I was positive I didn't want the answer, but just as sure that I needed it.

Mark looked around the room, and then licked the side of Liberty's face, from jaw to eyebrow. She grimaced and tried to pull away as I used the distraction her resistance provided to inch closer. He called a halt to both our actions by pressing the gun harder against her temple.

"Well, I've been watching you for a while, Dunstan. At first I was going to see what you were keeping locked up in that safe. But then you took off so fast I figured I'd follow you and find out what you were up to. I thought about killing you a few times, but there'd be no fun in that." He licked his lips. "Why should you get off easy? Killing you would be much too kind."

The psychopath used his unarmed hand to stretch the front of Liberty's dress away from her chest, while he gawked at her well rounded breasts. "Since you took it upon yourself to interfere with me and my women, I thought I'd return the favor." He nibbled on Liberty's ear and she shuddered.

"I know it's not a very fair trade, but honestly, you don't have much to offer. I'll take your girl."

"I am not his girl," Liberty growled through clenched teeth.

"No sweetheart, now you're mine." He leaned into her and smiled like they were posing for a picture. "Don't we look great together?"

"No," I held up my hand. "Listen, I'm sorry for what I did. Let me make it up to you."

"How are you planning to do that?" He tilted his head to the side. "Can you give me my life back? Can you call my mom and tell her that I was falsely accused? Can you buy me off?" He snarled. "No, this looks to be the best thing you have to offer right now, and I'm taking her for payback. Unless you want me to take her instead." He motioned toward the sleeping Ashley.

Liberty's green eyes grew as we shared a look of horror.

"Mark, please, I'm so sorry."

"You're right, you are." He leaned forward, faster than I expected, and my world grew black at the butt of his gun.

***March 1

"Jacob, I'm on my way," I said into the phone, trying to sound reassuring.

"We can't stay here," he replied. "We're heading to the store now, we'll meet—"

My phone went dead. I slammed the useless compilation of plastic and metal into my steering wheel.

I had been running on the treadmill in my home gym when I heard the news. Suddenly the basketball game I was watching switched to a "Live Breaking News Flash". When I saw the scene in front of the White House I tripped, and had to step to the side to avoid falling. I watched the television, disbelieving my eyes.

Americans were killing ... Americans.

I gathered up my guns, all the food in my house, and threw everything into my SUV. Dialing Jacob's cell, I peeled out of my driveway and headed his direction.

Jacob's wife was always prepared for a catastrophe. Cathy was one of those people who bought forty cases of bottled water and zip-dried food during Y2K. Over the last few months, as the recession plunged into a depression, she had been stocking up the safe in Jacob's store. They'd even had the safe door modified with a combo lock inside and out. I'd always considered her to be a little paranoid, but as I drove I reevaluated my opinion of my sister-in-law.

Jacob's store was five minutes from my house, but I made the drive in three. Traffic wasn't bad yet. People were probably still in shock, and I'd reacted faster than most would. Jacob clasped my hand and threw his other arm around me, squeezing me tight.

"You made it!" His pleased voice boomed throughout the small area of the safe. "I told you he'd make it, Cath."

Cathy walked over and embraced me. "Yes, dear, you did." She smiled at me. "I'm glad you're okay."

Uh-huh, sure.

I looked around and realized what was missing. "Where's Ashley?"

Cathy became agitated. "She isn't with you?"

"Sure she is." Jacob sounded confident as he smiled at me. "He'd never let anything happen to our little girl."

My glock appeared in my hand. Smoke rose from the warm barrel. "I killed you. Both of you." My eyes returned to their faces and bullet wounds appeared on their foreheads.

"You did what you had to. We for—" My brother and his wife faded away.

***June 16

"Uncle Connor, please wake up," Ashley begged.

Her tears spattered against my face, as she tried desperately to rouse me by tugging on my shirt.

"Ash, thank God you're okay." My shaky arms wrapped themselves around her before my eyelids opened.

She spoke to me!

I squeezed her, not wanting this moment to end, dreading the inevitable return of her silent treatment.

"Uncle ... Connor ... where ... is ... Libby?" Ashley asked slowly, emphasizing each word.

Where is Libby?

I closed my eyes and remembered Liberty's very large, very frightened eyes pleading with me to rescue her from the gun Mark Fletcher held to her head. I swallowed.

"She's gone." I held my forehead in my hand, trying to stop the throbbing. "My fault. But she'll be okay. I'll get her back." I massaged my temples for a minute, and then struggled to get to my feet. The throbbing in my head climaxed, becoming an obnoxious base line that turned my vision black. I gritted my teeth and stood against the pain. "He took her."

He will die.

"Took her?" Ashley grabbed my arm, attempting to steady me. "Who? Where? You're not making sense."

"Mark ... Fletcher had a gun ... took her." I pieced the facts together while heading toward the bed. Reaching between the mattresses, I pulled out my glock and its extra clip. Anger blurred my vision, and all I could see clearly was the memory of Mark's arms all over Liberty.

Ashley's slumped down on the bed. "I don't know what you're talking about! Who is Mark Fletcher? And where did he take her? And—"

"I don't know!" I snapped. "I just know I have to find her."

She ran to Liberty's pack. "I'm coming with you."

"You're what? I don't have time for this." I sat on the bed and put my wet shoes back on.

"I want to help. I'm coming." She rummaged through the pack and pulled out Liberty's gun and knife.

My jaw flew open. "No you're not. And put those down before you kill yourself!"

"So, what?" She glared at me. "I'm just supposed to wait here and hope you both come back? And what if he comes for me while you're gone?

"That's not—"

"I'm not going to just sit here and wait for you two to die!" Tears started forming in her eyes.

I looked around the room, desperate for help.

Ashley read my mind. "You don't have time to tie me up. We need to help Liberty." She wiped her eyes and sniffled.

"Okay fine." I glanced at the weapons in her hands. "You can come and bring the knife, but the gun stays."

She started to argue but I cut her off. "Ashley." I tried to sound composed. "You're barely twelve—you're not carrying a freaking gun!" I shook my head, refusing to believe I was even having this conversation.

My life used to be so normal.

16: Violations

Liberty

***June 15

I gasped as the intruder nailed Connor over the head with his gun. Connor crumpled to the floor like a rag doll.

Not dead. Please don't let him be dead.

Mark had one hand around my wrist, and the other on his gun, as he dragged me down the stairs. The front of my dress was stretched out, I had bite marks on my shoulders and chest, and my lip was bleeding.

This is why I don't date.

I watched my abductor from the corner of my eye.

Mark Fletcher? Seriously? How about sending a nice guy my way for a change?

Mark was infamous. Anyone who picked up a newspaper or turned on a TV during his trial knew who and what he was: spoiled rich boy turned sexual deviant. He preyed on young women, abused his position, and took advantage of his employees.

Mark found the duffle bag Conner had filled with food. He tucked his gun into his pants, unzipped the bag, and glanced inside. He grunted in approval, zipped it back up, and then slid it over my over my shoulder, slapping my butt like I was his own personal beast of burden. It stung and I reflexively stepped away, attempting to pull my wrist from his grasp.

My resistance only made him more forceful. He pulled me into his arms and nibbled on my earlobe. My back hit the wall as he pressed his body against mine. The air was so thick with his lust I could barely breathe.

"Just a taste," he purred and nibbled on my neck, starting in the center and moving to my ear. Anger danced with pain when he pierced my lobe between his teeth. I swung at him with my free hand, but he intercepted it. When I tried to kick him he moved closer, trapping my legs with his. I cried out, but he muffled my scream with his lips.

He ripped the clip from my hair. I gasped in pain and his tongue forced its way through my teeth. Coppery-sweet blood mingled with the flavor of Mark's kiss. Warm, sticky liquid dribbled down my neck as his hands pinned mine against the wall.

He pulled away from me and the manic gleam in his eyes shattered my fury—each shard of rage melted into a different shade of terror. As he led me from the house, the magnitude of my situation hit me. Mark was beyond reason and I was unarmed, with no allies, and no options.

Must run!

I lowered my shoulder and the bag fell to the ground with a loud thump. When Mark bent to pick it up I yanked my wrist from his grasp and sprinted away. It was a stupid move, but panic and intelligence are not usual bed fellows.

Mark caught me within seconds, grabbing a handful of my hair and jerking it hard, bringing me to a hasty stop. I fell backwards, arms flailing. My hands grasped for his jeans as I landed on my bottom with a tail-bone bruising thud. I battled for breath through my nose as he forced another disgustingly sloppy kiss on me. He dropped the duffel bag and pulled the gun out of his pants, returning it to my temple. His lips released mine and his hot, reeking breath stung my nostrils.

"You don't *need* to walk, and they don't *need* to live to get what I'm after." The threat was delivered with the sensuality of a lover and the malice of a serial killer; a disturbing combination.

He yanked my hair, pulling me back up to my feet, and led me over the threshold of a nearby house. This time I went willingly. There was no doubt in my mind of the consequences if I didn't. The door shut behind us—like the final nail in my coffin—extinguishing all hope.

"Sorry about this babe," he whispered into my ear.

A sharp pain on the side of my head preceded the nothingness that overcame me.

***June 16

I awoke, lying on my back. The room was dark, and I was cold and wet. I listened, hearing nothing but silence. The ceiling spun, and the shadows remained fuzzy, no matter how many times I blinked. My arms and legs were uncomfortable. I tried to reposition them, only to discover that I couldn't move.

Every inch of my body felt stiff and sore. I lifted my head and saw the problem: my hands and feet were secured by sheets, tied to bed posts. I tried to scream, but the sound was muffled by the gag in my mouth.

As my mind began to decipher previous events, my heart rate and throbbing head entered into a drumming competition. I gritted my teeth as each strived to beat louder and faster than the other. Out of all the ways I'd ever woken up, this was—hands down—the worst.

Seriously? We need to chat about Your sense of humor.

Though threatened several times, I'd never actually been gagged. It was a hideous experience that took helpless and violated to a whole new level. I pulled against the restraints to no avail; they held fast.

Oh yay. Our resident freak has apparently spent some time perfecting his bedroom bondage techniques. What a surprise.

By the time Mark's hazy figure darkened the doorway, my arms felt like they were being pulled out of their sockets. Human limbs were never meant to be in this position, and I had no idea how long I'd been there. It was still dark outside, but that told me nothing about the time, since the storm raged on. Each boom of thunder and flash of lightning created the ideal background for my personalized horror movie.

Mark slowly circled the bed—a predator inspecting his prey—then sat next to me. Pulling the gag down, he nibbled on my bottom lip, as I lay there, exposed. He kissed me again, but this time it was slow and tender. It might have even passed for romantic had he not knocked me out and dragged me to his kinky love nest against my will. I've heard that some women are into that sort of thing, but definitely not this one.

He came up for air and gave me a self-congratulatory smile. "I'm a better kisser than Dunstan, aren't I?"

I tried not to roll my eyes, but it was so typical. "I wouldn't know. I've never kissed Connor."

Mark backhanded me. It was so fast and unexpected that had my arms been free, I still couldn't have blocked in time. The slap felt like a belly-flop on my face. My eyes watered, my nose ran, and my pounding head stepped up the tempo.

"Don't lie." He glowered at me and raised his hand again. I winced, holding my tongue, not knowing how to respond. I lowered my eyes and tried to look cowed.

His hand dropped as he let out a breath. "I'm sorry. You just can't make me angry. I don't want to hurt you. If you make me hurt you again, I'll be very angry."

As my clouded brain searched for the logic in his muddled statement, he started pacing. "I had a good life before Dunstan came along. I bet he told you all about how he took me down." He paused and looked at me.

He's serious? He really thinks we sit around talking about him?

I hid behind my closed eyelids, hoping the maniac wouldn't find me there.

"He ruined my life!" Mark screamed the words. "I wasn't a saint, but neither was he. He had no right. He should have never intruded!"

I opened my eyes and watched him. If he was going to hit me again, this time I at least wanted to brace for the impact. It was too dark to see his expression, but anger emanated from his body in waves, eroding what was left of my resolve. Goosebumps spread across my flesh as I started to tremble.

He sat beside me and lovingly stroked the mark he'd left on my face. His touch brought sharp spikes of pain to my injured cheek. Raising his hand to his lips, he licked my blood from his fingertips.

Oh. God. Please help me.

"Hush. I won't let anyone hurt you. There's nothing to be afraid of." He tenderly brushed the hair away from my face.

I wanted to scream, but somehow retained the mental capacity to understand that it would be a very bad idea to evoke his anger again.

"Look at what he's turned me into." Mark's shoulders slumped. "I'm so sorry, sweetheart." He kissed my hair.

I didn't want to argue, but I had a pretty strong suspicion Mark had always been a power-hungry sex-fiend. So, with the blood he'd drawn running down my face, I tried to look as sympathetic and comforting as possible.

"It's never too late for you to prove everyone wrong. You don't have to be like this. You can be ... a good guy." I'd meant the words to be encouraging, but his expression immediately shifted from friendly to furious. Mark went nuclear, and I was at ground zero.

"What are they saying about me?" he shouted. "Have you spoken to my parents?"

I shook my head, "No, Mark. I've never met your parents. I ..."

Another hard slap stung my face, and this time I understood what it meant to see stars.

"Stop lying to me!"

Tears flowed freely down my cheeks with the realization that I was going to die at the hands of this monster.

Suddenly his face was an inch from mine. "What is the relationship of Dunstan and the girl?"

"I don't know. I just met up with them."

Before I had even finished speaking, Mark reached up my dress with his right hand and dug his thumb into my upper-inner thigh. The pain was excruciating as he pressed harder and harder, grinding back and forth between muscle, bone, and tendon. My bonds pulled tight with my effort to escape the torment.

"Please stop," I cried. "Stop! It hurts."

He moved his hand to my brachial pressure point and repeated the action. But this time the torture was accompanied by a demanding, vengeful kiss.

I closed my eyes and tried to escape the agony. Temporary reprieve came when Mark released me and dug into his pocket. His hand emerged and the faint glow of metal shone from the item he clutched. He pushed a button, and the blade flicked open.

"Please don't hurt me," I begged. "You promised you would take care of me!" I could feel the acceleration of my heart as adrenaline filled my veins.

When you can't fight and you can't fly, what good is adrenaline? What can you do?

"Oh honey." Mark's voice was strangely sympathetic. "You lied. You must be punished." His lips brushed my trembling forehead. He held the blade to my left cheek bone and slowly drew the knife toward my chin. I screamed as it bit into my flesh.

He paused, pulled his knife out and looked thoughtfully at the small wound. "No. He should be here to see this. He needs to witness the pain he's causing."

My voice turned hysterical as I thought of Ashley in Mark's hands. "No! Please! Don't leave me. Stay with me. You promised! You said you'd take care of me!" Dying here was bad enough, but the thought being mutilated in front of Connor and Ashley was more than I could bear.

He kissed my still protesting lips. "Hush. I'll be back soon, honey."

And then he was gone.

I gasped for air, shaking so violently that my teeth chattered. Deep down I knew I was selfish and welcomed the respite, even though it did not bode well for my companions. I had pleaded for him to stay, but in the end, I could not deny the relief that I felt when he left.

I am a horrible person.

Wanting to be better, I glanced around the room. There had to be some way to free myself and help Connor and Ashley—something I could do—a way to build a bomb from bubblegum. But I couldn't find anything. Frustrated, I growled, "Freaking MacGyver!"

Thunder boomed in the distance and lightning lit up the sky once more.

"This is not me. I am not the helpless idiot that ends up strapped to a bed."

A shot was fired outside.

The sound was more than I could handle. I screamed out my frustration, my fear, my self-loathing, and my helplessness. I wailed until my throat was sore.

When I regained control of my emotions, clarity filtered through my mind.

When you can't fight or fly, there's only one thing you can *do.*

I prayed.

17: Reunited

Liberty

Please God, don't let them be dead.

My eyes were squeezed shut while my lips muttered prayers. My right arm suddenly went slack. I opened my eyes, and saw Connor staring back at me. His expression went from concerned to furious when his glance lingered on my dress; pushed up around my hips. He quickly pulled it back down.

He thinks ...

"No Con—" I shook my head.

He grabbed a towel off the dresser and carefully wiped my face. "Ash, she's in here." He moved to my right foot, and cut the binding.

Morning was nearing. The room had lightened enough for me to make out Ashley's worried face as she rushed through the doorway. "Is she okay?" She looked up at Connor for a response.

"Me? Ash, I'm right here. You can talk to me."

Her eyes grew round when they found my face. "Sorry, I just ... sorry. Are you okay?"

My hands and feet had lost circulation when I'd struggled and tightened my bindings. As Connor cut the sheets, blood flowed to the numb appendages, like thousands of needles stabbing into my flesh. Connor moved back down to the foot of the bed and rubbed my bare feet.

I winced, and tried not to grit my teeth. "I'm okay. What about you two? I heard a gunshot."

"Uncle Connor shot him." Ashley's voice was somber, with a touch of something I couldn't place; almost like admiration.

I squirmed my feet away from Connor's grasp and scooted to the edge of the bed. I was upright for maybe a whole second before I collapsed.

Connor kneeled down and kneaded my feet again.

"I can do that." I felt my body tense as I tried to kick out of his grasp.

Connor ignored me, and held my legs still with little effort. His hands were warm and soothing as they massaged away the pain.

He helped me down the stairs. The first couple of steps were agonizing, but the man's magical hands had done wonders. We found my shoes and our stolen food bag, and headed toward the house we'd been staying in.

My fists were still cut up from my previous bout with the mirror. The right side of my face was swollen from Mark's heavy backhand. The cut on my left check stung, and leaked blood when I moved my jaw. My inner left thigh and bicep throbbed and would no doubt bare huge, purple bruises. The countless bite marks stung, my head pounded, and my whole body ached from being laid out like I was on the rack. I felt like an extra on the *Night of the Living Dead*" movie set.

Everything is fine. It could have been a lot worse. Nothing happened.

I went into the bathroom and shut the door behind me. The first thing I grabbed was a toothbrush. I poured a little water over it, covered the bristles in toothpaste, and vigorously scrubbed my teeth. Then I repeated the action three more times. My gums were bleeding by the time I was finished, but the taste of Mark lingered.

My face was a mess. The swelling on the right side was making it difficult to see. I wet the corner of a wash cloth and started scrubbing away blood. There was peroxide in the cabinet, so I cleaned up my ear and the cut on my cheek. Had the bottle been larger, I would have stood in the tub and poured it over me.

Pulling up the hem of my dress, I examined my inner thigh. The bruise was the size of a tennis ball, and rapidly purpling.

"I hate him." The words just tumbled out of my mouth before I could stop them with my hand.

No. I can't hate him. He's dead.

My eyes watered with sorrow, guilt, anger, fear, frustration, helplessness; emotional overload was an understatement.

A quiet knock sounded on the door. Ashley walked in and interrupted my futile thoughts, as I hastily lowered my dress.

Her eyes locked on mine, drifted downward, and then quickly went back to my eyes. We stared at each other as she opened and closed her mouth a few times.

"He didn't. I mean there was no ..." I had no idea how much to reveal about an almost-rape to a twelve year old. "Look, he just gave me a really bad bruise ... with his thumb." I pulled up my dress and showed her my inner thigh.

She came closer to examine my leg. "Ouch."

"Nothing but bruises and cuts happened."

She blew out a breath. "I didn't really think—"

"Yes, you did. I was tied up. *I* was scared it was going to happen."

"But you said you'd—"

"Put my knee through his genitals?" I winced, remembering the cockiness of my previous words. "He had my legs tied down. There was no way my knees were going to be of any help. I was wrong. I thought I was so strong, and I'm not. If you guys wouldn't have come for me, I'd ... I don't know."

Her face dropped as she stared at me like she'd just found out I couldn't walk on water.

"And hey, check out this one." I pushed up my sleeve to reveal my arm to her.

"Wow, colorful," she said admiringly.

"Yeah, they could have been a lot worse." I draped my arm over her shoulders. "Thanks, for coming for me."

"Uncle Connor was really worried about you. He tried to go after you without me. I had to beg him to bring me along."

"Oh." I chewed on my lip for a minute. "I figured you'd have to drag him behind you to save me again. Didn't I make him regret it enough the first time?"

Ashley giggled. "No, he was pretty upset."

"Funny," I said. "I never expected Connor Dunstan to be the hero-type, but that's twice now he's saved my life."

"Three times, actually." She held up three small fingers.

"I had that guy with the frying pan," I insisted. "But I guess we can give Connor points for effort."

"Yeah." She squeezed my hand. "Maybe he's not *all* bad."

Talking to Ashley helped greatly, but I was still shaking. I grabbed the brush off the counter, as I led the girl from the bathroom. We sat on the bed and I let down her hair, brushed out the tangles, and re-braided it. The comforting simplicity of fixing her hair did wonders to calm my nerves. By the time I finished, my breathing had steadied and my hands had almost entirely stopped trembling.

The affect on Ashley was even better. She was out cold by the time I pulled her braid through a rubber band. She leaned against my leg, finally giving in to sleep. I gently moved and lowered her to the bed.

"Pleasant dreams." I kissed her forehead as Connor entered the room.

He stepped over to the bed, picked up Ashley, and moved her to the pillow, pulling the covers up over her.

I stood and headed toward the dresser. Connor grabbed my arm and spun me back around to face him. His trembling arms wrapped me in an embrace that was both intrusive and comforting.

"I'm so sorry." He whispered into my hair.

"No need. Not your fault." I had no idea how to respond to his proximity.

"Yes, it was. He was after me. It wasn't your battle."

I gave in and nestled my head against his chest, wrapping my arms around him. I could hear his heart beat, and feel his incredible warmth. Part of me wanted to let my hands roam and explore the muscles under his shirt, but my sensible side screamed for me to be across the room from him.

Sensibility is so overrated.

I felt calm, relaxed and safe in his arms. I closed my eyes.

Mark's face popped into my mind. I gasped and stepped back, pushing Connor away.

His guarded expression returned.

"I'm sorry." I shook my head, trying to eradicate the memory. "I just—"

"It's okay, I get it." He let out a breath.

No you don't.

"I ... It isn't you."

"Do you want to talk about it?" The words sounded like he was trying them out for the first time.

"I don't ... he didn't ... I mean ... no ... sex." My shoulders tensed as I resented the necessity of the words.

Connor took a deep breath, visibly relaxing. He grabbed my hand and led me to the bed where he sat with his back against the wall and gestured for me to seat myself beside him. My expression was dubious as I considered his request.

Connor rolled his eyes. "All I want to do is talk."

Ashley is asleep right there. How dangerous could this be?

So I sat, with every intention of keeping at least six inches between us at all times. Connor sighed.

"What?" I asked.

"I won't bite."

My hand instinctively went to my bitten ear. The bleeding had stopped, but it was still tender. Connor reached for my hand and pulled it away, so he could inspect the damage. He swore, and then grabbed my waist and scooted me closer, turning my body so my back was against his torso.

I leaned against his warm, hard chest and guiltily enjoyed the comfort of his arms wrapped around me. The musky scent of metal, earth, and man that made up Connor soothed my mind. "It could have been a lot worse."

His arms tightened around me. "Yeah, it could have."

"His eyes were the worst part. When I looked into them, I knew he was going to kill me." A tear slid down my cheek. "And when he left, I was happy. Then I felt horrible, because he was coming for you guys."

"Shh. That's natural. You're not horrible. You were just afraid." He kissed the top of my head. "It's over now. Done. You don't have to think about it anymore."

I don't remember falling asleep, but every time the nightmares woke me, Connor's face was the first thing I saw. His breath on my cheek helped me forget about the taste of Mark's kisses. The light pressure of his arm resting against mine erased the memory of Mark's groping hands.

I had been arrogant, believing myself superior to "weaker women" who "allowed" themselves to be beaten or raped. I had smugly thought such a thing could never happen to me. But in the end, my ability to protect myself had been grossly inadequate. I was just as human as every other woman. Mark could have raped or killed me and I would have been powerless to stop him.

I slept through the next day and the night that followed. The time passed in a blur as I tossed and turned, restless and haunted by memories. Every time I opened my eyes, Connor was by my side, holding me.

18: Sick

Liberty

***June 18

The morning of the second day I finally got out of bed. We ate our last warm meal from the grill—canned clam chowder—and headed on our way atop the bicycles. The front tire of my bike was a little low, but other than that they were in great condition. We quietly rode the path around the golf course at a nice, steady pace.

Despite Ashley's previous concerns, she rode just fine, smiling as the slight wind played with her hair. The rain had stopped, but the ground was still damp, and earth worms slithered across the road. Ashley ran over one and muttered, "Ewwe."

Connor laughed and set out to run down all of the worms he could find to capitalize on Ashley's disgusted reaction. It was easy to push aside the recent trauma while we enjoyed the fresh, new day. The sun crept from behind the clouds, choreographed to the chirping of the birds. Just an average family, enjoying a morning bike ride, we laughed and joked for almost a half hour before we rounded the last turn.

From the moment the clubhouse came into view, I knew something was amiss. Unexplainable but equally undeniable bad vibes seemed to roll off the siding. The building was creepy to the nth degree.

Connor waved us to a stop behind a group of trees. He watched the clubhouse as we huddled close to him.

"This place gives me the creeps," I whispered.

Connor nodded. "We're gonna have to skirt around the main area. Stay on the path." He put his foot back on the pedal, preparing to take off.

"Wait." I held up my hand. "Maybe we should ride through the grass around it?"

Connor shook his head. "The ground is wet and the grass is too long. These aren't mountain bikes."

"We could just walk them?" I really didn't want to go as close to the building as the path would take us.

Connor thought for a moment, and then shook his head again. "I have a bad feeling about this. We ride. We have to be able to get away fast, should the need arise."

Normally I would argue just to be contrary, but there was something about his demeanor that kept me from questioning his orders. His natural leadership skills were remarkable enough to make even me hold my tongue.

He looked me over. "Where's your gun?" I dug through my pack, retrieved it, and started to tuck it into the back of my pants.

"Take the safety off."

I did as he requested and slipped it into the waistband of my jeans. Connor had been carrying the extra duffel bag of supplies over his shoulder. He wrapped the straps securely around the handlebar of his bike, freeing up his arms.

"Everyone ready?" He put his foot on the pedal and pushed off, without waiting for a response.

Ready for what?

As our bikes slowly rolled forward, I couldn't shake the feeling that I was the stupid girl in some horror flick; biking toward my doom while the audience yelled at me to go the other way. The sensation was stronger than a premonition, but it wasn't the *call*.

In the stillness, we heard what was happening behind the clubhouse long before we saw it. The disturbance sounded like someone was splitting wood—only different. It was too late to turn back, so we continued our apprehensive approach.

When they came into view, it took me a minute to decipher what I was seeing. Once comprehension set in, my resolve was tested at the sight of three men methodically butchering the corpse of another. Ashley gasped, and then her hand flew to her mouth.

Three savage faces turned toward her, like a pack of wild wolves eyeballing a rabbit.

Ashley perfected the role of frightened hare and froze in terror. Her mouth hung open; her expression a mixture of shock and disgust.

The sound of a gunshot woke me from my own stupor. One of the men went down. I looked up to see Connor aiming the gun for a second shot. I started to object. This wasn't self defense, it was murder! We didn't know the details, and we couldn't just walk up and start shooting people. But my protest froze on my lips as the other two men sprang toward us.

"Ash, come on, we have to get out of here!" I pleaded desperately, but she was completely immobile.

Connor fired again, taking the second man in the chest.

It all happened so fast, and before I could blink the third man was almost upon Ashley. I ran in front of her as my trembling hands reached for my gun. I wasn't going to be quick enough—he was too fast. The gun slipped out of my hand. A bloody knife came straight for me.

I closed my eyes, bracing for the inevitable.

Another shot rang out.

I heard the impact of the bullet, and then felt warm liquid cover me. I wiped my eyes, and then opened them. Connor's shot had literally taken the man's head off. I stared at my hands as blood dripped from them.

"Oh my—" It was all I could get out before I leaned over and emptied my stomach.

My world swayed and my vision darkened.

Breathe.

Connor had woken Ashley from her trance and encouraging her legs to pedal.

"Time to go, Libby. Now."

"I'm freaking trying!" I yelled back, vexed by the fact that he sounded so calm when I had someone else's blood dripping from my face.

A nightmare. No way is this real, just get out of here and wake up.

I turned, retrieved my gun and climbed back on my bike as additional people rushed out of the clubhouse. All four of them fell to Connor's gun before I even started pedaling. He calmly replaced his empty clip with a full one, climbed back on his bike, and took off. I stared after him in awe.

Who is this guy?

Connor slowed until I passed him, and then he kept watch behind us. We rode hard until we reached the East Valley Highway. Ashley's color slowly started coming back, but she still hadn't spoken a word. I was worried, but didn't feel that approaching her while covered in gore was a good idea. I stopped my bike, leaned the frame against my leg, and searched my pack for a rag and a water bottle.

"What are you doing? We have to keep moving." Connor stopped his bike and stared at me.

"I have to get it off now." I doused the towel with water. Realization hit that I was about to wipe someone else's face off my own. When I raised the rag, I lost control of my hands and they shook wildly.

"I can't get it off!" I squirmed and my bike slid to the ground, tripping me as it fell. I tried to catch myself on the frame, but my hand slipped off and I ended up on my hands and knees, intertwined in the frame of my bike.

Connor grabbed my arm before I had the chance to shout any colorful obscenities. He untangled my limbs and hoisted me up.

"Let me help you." He took the wet rag from me.

I nodded and closed my eyes—as tears welled up and threatened to fall. I was a quivering, sniveling mess, and Connor was calm and collected after shooting the head off a man who'd been less than a foot from me.

"Talk to me Libby." He sounded worried, but his steady hands worked fast and efficiently. "You're tense. Heart's pounding. You need to calm down."

"Y-Y-You shot a man right in front of my face!" My hands wrapped themselves around my stomach as I rocked back and forth on my heels. "I am wearing another person!" I shuddered as my gorge threatened to rise again.

I opened my eyes and scowled at Connor. "And you! You could have killed me. And you want me to *calm down*?"

He grabbed my chin and forced my eyes to meet his. "I know what I'm doing. Now close your eyes."

I complied and he gently ran the rag over my eyelids.

"Obviously." My shoulders slumped and the shaking lessened. "We're alive and they're dead. Who are you, anyway?" Connor was trying to get I-don't-even-want-to-know-what out of my hair. "Lawyers do *not* shoot like that."

"Uncle Connor was in the army." Ashley surprised us both when she spoke.

He turned toward her and she shrugged. "You knew about that?"

"Dad carried your army picture in his wallet."

"Army? Why didn't you tell me?" I studied the man, wondering what other secrets he kept.

He looked at the ruined, bloody rag and tossed it into the ditch on the side of the road. "Why didn't you ask?"

"Never mind. I don't even care." I picked up my bike. "Right now, all I want to do is shave my head and bathe in bleach."

"Right." He nodded as he climbed on his own bike. "Then let's get out of here."

Putting some serious miles between us and the clubhouse of death seemed like a very good idea. Working under the delusion that we could outrun the nightmares, we pedaled hard.

During our flight, my mind tried to connect what I knew with what I saw. I knew that the lives we'd just taken had once been human; with families, jobs, dreams, ambitions, and feelings. But what I saw proved the possibility that people could no longer be human.

I looked at my adopted family and silently prayed that the same would never happen to us.

The plan was to skirt around Auburn, and then take Highway 18 northeast, skipping most of Seattle's populated outskirts. Then we'd hit Highway 203 to Monroe.

There was such a long way to go that to plan further was futile. We tried to focus on the immediate task at hand, to avoid being discouraged about the long term. The depressing reality was that even Monroe was a significant distance, and if we made it that far it would be a miracle.

We biked for about six hours and felt the effects. Ashley's bike started leaning to the right and I was afraid she'd fall asleep mid-pedal.

"Connor." I nodded toward the girl.

He studied Ashley's movements for a moment and nodded. "There's some houses up on the right."

I raised an eyebrow at him. "You look a little beat yourself."

The side of his mouth twitched. "I'm not even gonna say what you look like."

"You're such a jerk, Connor."

"What? I didn't even say it."

We stashed the bikes under a nearby bush and entered the house to investigate. No death smells, no disgustingly disfigured bodies, and no one eating anyone else. I took a deep breath through my nose and enjoyed the absence of menacing odors.

It's all about finding joy in the little things.

The house was a one level bungalow, probably built in the early sixties and never redecorated. The walls were covered in shades of green better left to vegetables, and the orange shag carpet had never been a good idea. I could picture my own grandparents living very comfortably in such a home. Family photos and knick-knacks covered the walls and all available surfaces of the place. Magazines for every interest were laid out on the coffee table. A stack of newspapers rested beside a big, comfy-looking lazy boy.

After we brought the bikes in and locked all the doors Ashley found her voice.

"They were eating other people, weren't they?" A look of absolute horror consumed her face.

I chewed on my lip to prevent myself shouting, "Soylent Green is people!" Cannibalism was well outside my list of appropriate conversation topics. So instead of attempting to lighten the mood, I squirmed before the inquiry in Ashley's eyes, wishing they were focused elsewhere.

Luckily Connor saved me from responding when he draped his arm around the girl and squeezed her tightly. "I'm not gonna lie to you—there are bad people out there, Ash. But we're different. We're stronger and smarter." He kissed the top of her head and brushed away stray hairs. "And we're a team."

My jaw dropped as I stared at him.

Who are you and what did you do with Connor?

"Uncle Connor, Libby ..." Ashley's big, dark eyes glanced back and forth between us as she took each of our hands. "Thank you ... for taking care of me."

My heart swelled, and just like that I knew we were going to be okay. We were going to survive. We could persevere and beat the craziness, the loneliness, and the starvation. We'd become a family, and we would weather the storms together.

19: Travels

Liberty

Stale granola was dinner that night. We found it in the cupboards of the bungalow and nibbled on handfuls while stumbling into the master bedroom. I searched through the closet, trying to find the least "granny" shirt I could to replace my gore covered top.

I'd already wasted a bottle of water cleaning myself off and since we were away from the river, I was hesitant to squander anymore. But sleeping with body parts in my hair was not an option. I dumped just enough water on my head to loosen up the chunky areas and combed it out.

We piled onto the queen bed, and slipped promptly into an exhaustion provoked blackout.

***Lakeview, Oregon, fourteen years ago

2:58 pm: the dashboard clock glowed mockingly.

'Two minutes! I am so dead!' I grumbled into the steering wheel of my mom's Toyota Camry, pleading with her—my sisters and I were convinced that the car was female—to somehow make the ten minute drive in two minutes. The Camry had never shown signs of teleportation abilities before, but I was desperate.

'Come on Bessie, you can do it." I hoped the use of the car's pet name would spark her superpowers. We called her Bessie because she ran like an old milk cow, but now probably wouldn't be the best time to bring that up.

2:59.

My mom was working, and had given me specific instructions to be home by three o'clock. Our house had a water leak, and a man from the city was scheduled to fix it. If no one was there to let him in we'd be put back on a waiting list for another month—with another outrageous water bill.

And Mom would kill me.

But even worse than death, she'd take away my license for a month.

Michelle and I had been enjoying the gorgeous summer day. Hanging out at the public swimming pool, dipping our feet in the cool water, and checking out the hot life guards passed the time entirely too quickly.

3:00.

I could cut through the parking lot of Stratton's Grocery Store and shave two minutes from the drive. It wasn't exactly legal, but we all did it. I barely brushed the brake as I turned the steering wheel into the lot.

'*NO!*' the call ordered, but for the first time I ignored the voice in my heart.

There wasn't time to get back on the road, and I was already committed to the shortcut. I might still be able to catch the man. I gripped the steering wheel and stepped on the gas.

An indecipherable shape suddenly appeared in front of my car. I slammed on the breaks. There was a heart-stopping thump; evidence of impact. Everything went blurry. The next thing I knew, I was standing in front of Bessie, staring down at the bicyclist I'd just hit. I held my breath as one bike tire continued to spin.

"Oh my God, You killed him!" the manager of the store screamed as she hurried over.

"Someone, call the paramedics," another voice yelled. "A boy's been hit!"

My hand flew to my mouth and all time stopped.

A crowd gathered around the small figure, whispering, shaking heads, and waiting for the child to move ...

***

I awoke with a jolt. With the memory came tears. Always.

I remember. I promise.

Connor was gone, but Ashley was still asleep beside me. I slipped into the bathroom and quietly closed the door behind me. I gripped the counter and leaned into the mirror. My eyes were as haunted as my spirit. I squeezed them shut and saw the spinning bike tire. The fear I'd felt that day returned as I slunk to the floor, tucking my knees under my chin and wrapping my arms around my legs.

My heart and mind wandered back to the emergency room, where I paced and prayed while paramedics worked on little Mike Fredrickson. His mother was the first to arrive, showing up in her work slacks and silk shirt with her graying hair neatly pulled into a bun. She stared at me for a long minute, and then burst into tears. News travels fast in a small town, and she'd no doubt heard several versions of the incident already.

"Mrs. Fredrickson—" I stepped forward, but she held up her hand, turned, and walked toward the admittance desk. I sat in the furthest corner I could find with my knees drawn to my chest. I closed my eyes and hid behind my legs as tears started to fall.

Are You still there? I'm sorry. I should have listened. I really screwed up. Please, just let Mikey be alright. I promise I'll never ignore You again. I'll listen. I'll do whatever You want. Please. He's just a kid. Please don't let him die. Don't let him be paralyzed. Please let him be okay.

Others came and went, casting sideways glances in my direction.

"Isn't that Rose Collins' daughter?" I heard someone whisper.

"Rose Collins?" asked another voice.

"That woman works too much," a third chimed in.

"Never has any time for her children," the second said with a huff.

"Can't find a man?" asked a new voice.

"Who's gonna want to take on three troublesome girls?"

Their voices blended together as my head spun.

Now I've done it for sure. We'll have to move.

A tap on my arm caused me to raise my head and open my eyes.

"Shell." Tears ran down my cheeks at the sight of my best friend. "I swear it was an accident. I didn't see him. I wouldn't ..."

"I know." She sat down and draped her arm over my shoulders. The presence of my ally relaxed me, allowing me to embrace my fear and sorrow, and truly cry for what I had done.

The doctor came out and the family gathered around him. When he left, I stood and approached Mikey's mom with Michelle close behind.

"Excuse me, Mrs. Fredrickson. How is he?" I fiddled with the hem of my shirt.

All eyes focused on me, but no one said a word.

"Please." I crossed my arms. "I'm sorry. I just want to know if he's okay."

A plump, dark-haired woman stepped in front of Mrs. Fredrickson and stuck her finger in my face. "Of course he's not okay. You tried to kill him."

My jaw dropped and my mouth hung open, but no air reached my lungs. "I ... It was an accident." They glowered at me with such hatred I wanted to crawl into a hole and die. "I ... I didn't mean—"

I felt a hand on my shoulder and everyone's attention shifted behind me. I looked back and saw my mother. Her jaw was set and her eyes were the color of steel. She worked in a sawmill, and always smelled of wood, sweat and love.

"Momma, I'm sorry." I stared at her, but she wasn't looking at me. She was glaring over my head.

"My daughter asked how Michael is doing." She clenched her fists.

Mrs. Fredrickson cleared her throat. "He's going to be okay." Her gaze dropped to the floor and oxygen finally found its way to my lungs.

Mikey ended up with a broken arm, three cracked ribs and a sprained ankle. They said it would have been much worse had he not been wearing his helmet. I *could* have killed him.

I swear I will never ignore you again.

***June 19

We ate dry ramen from our packs for breakfast, climbed on the bikes, and cycled for about 9 miles, through the city of Auburn. Auburn was a typical smaller college city, hiding in Seattle's shadow. The downtown area consisted mainly of older buildings. Several of which were mom and pop shops that had been hit the hardest by the rough economy. Large "OUT OF BUSINESS" signs accompanied boarded windows and doors distinguished those that fell before the riots. Some buildings had been torched, but the level of destruction here didn't even compare to what I'd witnessed in Olympia.

The whisper of life was evident in the occasional flicker of a curtain or creak of a loose floor board. We kept to ourselves, and no one bothered us.

We stopped to stretch just north of Auburn's college. My sore legs were happy to take a break from riding, and if Ashley's bow-legged waddle was any indication, she felt the same. Connor continued to annoy me by showing no visible side effects from the ride.

Jerk.

The grassy area we stopped at served as a gathering spot for all sorts of birds, squirrels, and ducks, whose conversations created a Disney-type reality. The seven dwarves could come whistling by at any moment, but I feared that with our luck it would most likely be evil stepmothers and wicked witches.

I contemplated taking off my socks and shoes to feel the grass under my feet as a naive covey of quail wandered over to investigate us. Never one to pass up an opportunity, I calmly reached down and grabbed a large stick. Weapon in hand, I held still and waited for one gullible quail to waddle up to me. I didn't have to wait long.

She swings, she hits!

Down went the quail. Its companions scattered, but not before Connor clobbered a second one with the stick he'd picked up to follow my lead. One more quail died; the result of a combined effort as Connor chased it my direction and I made contact.

"Thank you softball practice." I dropped my weapon to the ground.

We grabbed the three quail we'd bashed and headed back toward the bikes.

"Gross! What are you doing with those?" Ashley's expression looked torn between laughter and horror.

My mouth twitched. "Seriously? You've never had quail? You, my dear, are in for a treat."

Connor coughed to cover his chuckle as Ashley eyed us suspiciously.

We followed Highway 18 about twelve more miles and found ourselves in the woods. Washington forests are a comforting compilation of bright, healthy shades of green and fresh, clean scents of earth and life. The feeling of serenity that overcomes me when I enter these wooded havens is invigorating.

Hidden by the enormous evergreens, we agreed this would be the best place to cook the quail. I headed toward the sounds of a nearby stream as Connor and Ashley scavenged for firewood.

As I approached the stream, an amazing sense of calm settled over me, mending the wounds of my recent trials. I closed my eyes and basked in the sounds and fragrances of life around me.

To my left, two squirrels engaged in a heated discussion. One took off up a tree and his antagonist followed. I imagined *Chip* raising his fist and screaming at *Dale*.

A smile tugged at my lips; one part reminiscent, two parts disheartened. Michelle and I used to translate wildlife conversations for her father. I closed my eyes and remembered my friend's contagious laughter.

I'd purchased my passport so I could visit Michelle, but never made it to Canada.

I glanced at my hands, and my mother's ring reminded me that I'd neglected her as well. Momma had begged me to come home this past Christmas, but the layoffs had already begun, and I couldn't get away.

What I wouldn't do for one more shot at Christmas ...

By the time I got back with the plucked and washed quail, the fire was going strong. Ashley and Connor had their heads together, deep in conversation.

I coughed, making my presence known.

Ashley jumped, looking decidedly guilty. "'Bout time. I'm starving."

Hmm. Wonder what those two are up to now.

"Good. Now warsh up. I'ma teach yah ta cook so as y'll make some lad a good wife, I recon." My southern accent was pathetic.

Ashley giggled. "You're so weird."

I cut large chunks of quail meat from the bones, placed them into the skillet, and covered them with water. Once the lid was secured, I balanced the pan on some burning tree limbs.

"You're boiling it?" Connor eyed the skillet skeptically.

"Quail is better if you boil it for awhile. Tenders it right up." My reply was polite, even though I wanted to yell at him to mind his own business and stay out of my kitchen.

While the meat was boiling, Ashley and I gathered a few small sticks and whittled one side of each to a point. Once the quail was no longer pink in the middle, we used the trimmed sticks as skewers. I sprinkled salt, pepper and rosemary on each chunk of meat. Then we held the sticks over the fire, like marshmallows, until the meat sizzled and browned.

Our labors produced mouth-watering smells and scrumptious tastes. The boiling had indeed tenderized the meat, and roasting it over the open fire made the outside slightly crispy; a juicy, delicious perfection. Some veggies would have perfected the dish, but it was still quite literally the best meal I'd had in a long time.

Ashley was a little hesitant at first, but the intoxicating aroma convinced even her. She closed her eyes, and I watched her expression as her taste buds exploded in culinary ecstasy. A big self-congratulatory smile spread across my face, and I was in danger of breaking my arm to pat myself on the back when Connor spoke.

"I always wanted to marry a cook." His big, dark eyes studied me, daring me to react.

Fear humbled me immediately, and I tried to cover it up with a look of contempt. "Not this cook. Not even if you were the last man on earth, Mr. Dunstan."

Connor's gaze bore into me, making my knees knock. He sized me up like a witness he was about to cross-examine. Arching an eyebrow, the corner of his mouth curved up in a very devious smirk. "Is that a challenge, Miss Collins?"

Gulp.

20: Bikes

Liberty

Our bicycle transportation was a blessing and I wondered why I hadn't thought of it sooner. We followed Highway 18 for three days, turned north on Highway 203, and continued for another three days. We'd been averaging about ten miles a day on the bikes, stopping often to hunt, fish or forage. When houses weren't available, or didn't seem safe, we slept under bushes or in barns. We ate whatever we could find and raided supplies whenever we got the chance.

I was hunted, feeling very much like a vulnerable mouse. And with every predatory smile Connor flashed me, he enforced his position as the lion; stalking my heart with every turn of his head. Now that he and Ashley were speaking, her words and actions showed that she was more than willing to shove me into the maw of the beast. Entirely too often I'd catch them with their heads together in a conspiratorial whisper.

"Ash, are you sure your stomach is okay?" I asked after her third particularly long bathroom break of the day. "I mean your potty breaks have tripled since you started talking to Connor. Why do I get the feeling someone's playing match maker?" I raised an eyebrow at her. "Please tell me you're not doing that."

She smiled sweetly.

Uh-oh. I massaged my temples and closed my eyes.

"I ... I ... He said he just wanted to talk to you." She fidgeted and scanned the area. "He wants to get to know you better. It's so sweet, Lib."

I shook my head and chuckled as flattered and terrified battled to determine which would be my position on the matter. "Ash, I thought you were my girl? How can I trust you to have my back if you're plotting against me?"

She's just a kid, doing what she was told.

She nodded. "I'm sorry, Lib. I didn't think you'd be upset." She stared down at her feet and I felt like a heel.

I put my finger under her chin and raised it, forcing her eyes to find mine, I smiled. "I'm not upset. You're a sweetheart, Ash. Love ya girly."

She dimpled. "Love ya too."

***June 25

We stopped a few miles south of Monroe, at a duck infested shoal of the Skykomish River. There were feathered meals everywhere, so we parked our bikes and approached slowly. At the edge of the river I crouched down, taking my pack off my shoulders.

"What are you doing?" Connor squatted beside me.

I turned my pack upside down, holding the items inside with one hand. Crumbs tumbled out. There weren't many morsels in the bottom of my pack, but it was more than enough to gain the attention of every duck on the water—and probably for a five mile radius. They honked, quacked, and flapped their feathers, charging us like a bunch of moms racing toward the best deal of a Black Friday sale.

Ashley screamed and ran for her bike.

I was tempted to do the same, but hunger provided me with a sudden and unexpected burst of courage. I whipped out my dagger and faced the horde of frightening fowl. Connor did the same, and between the two of us, we took down one Canadian goose and two ducks before they realized the danger and scattered.

We picked up our kills and were carrying them back to the bikes, when Connor stopped and held his finger to his mouth. His head tilted to the side for a second, and then dropped the goose he held and drew his gun. He ran toward a bush a few yards away to the left of Ashley and disappeared.

Ashley and I looked at each other, and then studied the bushes. I motioned for her and she ran to me.

"Did you hear anything?" I pulled out my gun as she approached.

"I don't know. How can anyone hear anything over those?" She pointed toward the dead ducks in my hands.

Connor reappeared and walked toward us; brow furrowed and body tense.

I raised an eyebrow. "What is it?"

He turned and stared back at the direction he'd come from. "I'm not sure." Bending down, he retrieved the honker he'd dropped. "But we should get out of here just to be safe."

By the time we made it to the outskirts of Monroe, I was riding on the rim of my deflated front tire. I patted the handle bars of my bike. "You can do it, Pinky, that's a good, little, sissy-bike."

Ashley giggled. "I don't think that's going to help."

"I know, but look." We were almost to Main Street, and I could see a small store across the road with a sign that read 'Bob's Bike Shop.'

The store looked harmless enough from the outside. The front window was broken, but the vandalism matched the surrounding buildings. We made our way inside and examined the remaining inventory.

"What do you think about this one?" I pulled a men's bike down from the top rack.

"Black?" Ashley asked. "I like this one." She pointed to the pink bike by her knee.

"Pink? Seriously? Do I look like a girl who likes pink?"

She giggled. "Purple?" She pointed to the equally girly-bike beside the pink one.

I sighed dramatically as I swung my leg over the black, K2 mountain bike. "What's wrong with black?"

The sound of a shotgun being cocked behind us interrupted our girl-bonding, shopping day.

I immediately surrendered, raised my hands above my head, and slowly turned around to see ...

"Wow." The word escaped through my lips as I stared at the woman before me.

Our rifle wielder looked like she just stepped out of a Macy's clothing store. Black, fitted jeans hugged her slim but shapely figure and flowed over black boots. Her ideal chest was accentuated by a red, fitted scoop neck top. Her shiny, brown hair was cut stylishly into a chin-length bob. She looked clean and smelled of expensive perfume.

My own frizzy-yet-greasy curls were trying to escape the braid I'd fashioned to restrain them, and I was acutely aware of the odor coming from my body.

Frosty blue eyes highlighted by the perfect amount of dark liner roved from my black frayed t-shirt to my dirty, rugged jeans, to my worn sneakers, and then back up to my battered face. I was quite a bit taller, but somehow she managed to look down her nose at me, snorting in disgust.

I had been dismissed.

"What are you doing in my shop?" She stared out at us over the double-barreled shotgun.

I glanced out the window at the large sign that had drawn my attention. "So, you're ... Bob?"

The corner of her lip shaped into a sneer as Connor appeared behind her and pressed his glock against the back of her head.

"They're bike shopping, Bob. Put down the gun, nice and easy." Connor took a step closer to her.

She didn't move.

"You'll want to put it down," Connor insisted. "Yours is more powerful, but mine is faster."

I didn't snicker. Not quite.

She lowered the shotgun, raised her hands in the air, and gradually turned toward Connor. He kicked the rifle away.

Her voiced turned sultry when the stranger recognized my companion. "Oh my. Connor Dunstan, right?"

I rolled my eyes as a smile spread across his face.

There was a rustling sound, followed by footsteps to my left. We all glanced in the direction to see a man aiming a semi-automatic at Connor. He was dressed in cargo-style camo pants and a black, sleeveless t-shirt. There was a tribal band tattoo wrapped around his well defined, right bicep. His hair was dark and cut short, revealing the small stud that sparkled in his left earlobe. He had that rebellious, bad-boy look about him that reminded me of Matt Damon in the *Bourne* movies. I eyed the newcomer wondering if he was as competent and deadly as *Jason Bourne* had proven himself to be.

Connor grabbed the woman's arm and pulled her between himself and the newcomer. He kept his gun aimed at her head, as he and the man stared each other down. Guns raised, muscles flexed, testosterone levels flaring, the situation had every potential to end in tears.

"Put the gun down, Jeff." The woman sounded calm as she spoke to the newcomer.

"I will when he does." Jeff continued to scrutinize Connor.

The woman sighed. "Don't you recognize him? He's that famous attorney from Olympia. He isn't a murderer. Right, Connor?"

Connor held very still. "I'm willing to talk."

Jeff gave a stiff nod.

"There." The woman smiled. "Everyone agrees to play nicely."

Eyes still locked, they slowly lowered their weapons. No one made a sound nor drew a breath. When they stood back up, their firearms remained on the floor.

The woman turned to face Connor, holding out her hand to him. "My name's Gina." She nodded to the man. "Jeff is my brother."

As Connor gripped her hand, her smile seemed a little suggestive.

I cleared my throat. Ashley and I might as well have been invisible. "I'm Liberty. This is Ashley, and you already know Connor."

She glanced at me again with a look that said she was clearly unimpressed.

My jaw tightened in response.

"Now then." She turned her attention back to Connor. "There hasn't been anyone around here for over a week. You frightened us."

He shuffled his feet. "Sorry. Got a flat tire. Just need a replacement."

Gina looked thoughtful as she considered Connor. "We've been looking for traveling companions. Which direction are you heading?"

Connor's glance shifted from Gina, to Jeff, back to Gina. "North."

I was standing to the side, so I saw the look that Gina and Jeff shared—like a heated argument with their eyes. His jaw clenched and she smiled in victory.

"Jeff and I planned to head to Canada, once we found Dad."

"Gina—" Jeff shifted his feet.

She held up a hand in his direction. "No Jeff, obviously he's not coming back. Maybe he's up there waiting for us. This is our chance." She turned her smile back on Connor. "If the gentleman is kind enough to let us tag along."

Gentleman?

Connor crossed his arms and leaned back on his heels. "We can trust you?"

"No more than we can trust you. But there is safety in numbers, and we can all benefit from an alliance." She intensified the suggestive nature of her words by placing her hand on Connor's arm.

He nodded. "I'm listening."

"We have provisions." She gestured toward a couple of bags leaning against the wall. "Jeff is a hunter, and you are obviously a survivor. Even with a woman and child tagging along." She smiled at him. "That's so sweet."

I coughed.

Too easy. Too convenient. Too irritating.

Connor's glance shifted between Gina and Jeff several times before he finally nodded. "If either of you try anything, I'll kill you both." He delivered the words without emotion.

I ground my teeth, but if Connor heard the noise, he ignored it. Ashley and I had been pushed into the background as he decided what was best for us.

"Connor, can I talk to you for a second?" My hands went to my hips as I glared at him.

"Later," he said, without even a glance in my direction.

The side of Gina's mouth curved up into a wicked smirk. *He'll pay for this.*

Weapons were retrieved, fresh bikes were selected and we all took off heading northeast on Highway 2. Gina and Connor rode together leaving Jeff, Ashley, and I to follow behind them. Connor continued to ignore my presence, keeping his gaze focused on Gina. Compared to the rose, I felt like a weed. I listened as Connor and Gina talked incessantly.

"The last time I saw you on the news was that trial ... The one where that guy sold the plans to that airliner." Gina glanced at Connor. "Right?"

Connor smiled his famous, blood-sucking smile. "That was just an allegation. My client was cleared of all charges."

Connor Dunstan: valiant defender of the guilty.

I rode between Jeff and Ashley, like riding in the back seat with the kids. But none of us kids were happy about the status. We pedaled in silence, glaring holes into the backs of the two ahead of us.

After a couple of hours, Jeff wheeled his bike closer to mine. "Stop torturing yourself."

Scowling took all of my concentration and Jeff's cryptic words were an annoying distraction. "What?"

"Gina always gets her way." He nodded toward the chatting couple. "Might as well kiss your boyfriend goodbye now."

I stopped glaring at Connor's back long enough to give Jeff an indifferent glance. "He's not my boyfriend."

"Right." He nodded. "I didn't really think he was, but it happens all the time." He shrugged. "When Gina glows, everyone else pales."

I glanced at Gina and let out a breath. "She is very pretty." I looked over at Jeff and he beamed me an impressive smile. His baby-blues lit up like headlights. "But you're a good-looking guy. Surely *you* don't disappear into your sister's shadow?"

He blushed. It was slight and ever so cute, making me feel like a cougar, eyeballing a young buck. I had to be at least ten years his senior.

Ashley closed the space between us and joined the conversation.

"So ..." I turned toward Jeff. "What was your previous life like?"

The side of his mouth twitched in a sad smile. "School and work."

"Where were you going to school?" I asked.

"University of Pudget Sound." He ran a hand through his hair, and then replaced it on the handlebar.

"UPS? That's where my friend Katie went." I glanced at Jeff. "Liberal arts school, right?"

He nodded and pursed his lips together.

I rolled my eyes, frustrated by his lack of willingness to give details. "Well ... What did you major in?"

Some people just don't know how to communicate.

"Social sciences." His barely audible reply was voiced while he stared at the ground in front of him.

I blinked. "Social—"

"Yeah." Gina's scornful voice cut in. "Social sciences. Jeff wanted to be a substance abuse counselor."

Ashley and I shared confused glances. "That's ... a bad thing?"

Gina turned her glare toward me. "I wouldn't expect *you* to understand." She turned back around to Connor and they continued their conversation while I gaped at her back.

Did she just—?

"Liberty." Jeff interrupted my fuming. "It's alright."

He slumped over his bike. Just like that Gina had crushed his Jason Bourne confidence.

"Why do you let her do that to you?" I glared at the back of Gina's head.

Jeff shrugged. "She's my big sister. And she's ... Gina."

I sighed. "Yeah, well she's not *that* pretty."

Connor called us to a stop beside a small spring. He slid his bike under a bush on the side of the road, and walked back to us as Gina hid her bike.

He glanced from Jeff to me and spoke. "I need the ducks."

A please would be nice.

I stood, with my bike still between my legs, and blinked like a simpleton.

He gritted his teeth. "I'm going to cook the ducks. I need them."

I wondered if I should start drooling to complete my idiot guise.

"Please?"

"*You're* going to cook them?" I pulled my pack off my shoulders and unzipped it. "You?"

He glanced at Jeff as I handed him the birds. "Of course." He motioned for Ashley to follow him. "Bring the pan and come on."

Ashley looked at me, shrugged, stashed her bike, and followed Connor.

Jeff chuckled. "Nice guy."

I sighed. "He used to be. I don't understand what's going on with him now." I kicked my leg over my bike and my jeans got caught in the chain. The bike wobbled as I jumped on one foot trying to balance my weight and untangle my pants at the same time.

Jeff's bike hit the ground. He wrapped one arm around my waist and steadied my bike with the other.

Wow, can I not even get off a bike without bruises?

"I am the world's biggest klutz." My face turned red as I finally kicked my leg free.

"Nah." Jeff took the bike from me and hid it. "You're just tired."

I attempted a smile that no doubt looked more like a grimace.

Exhausted.

Ashley showed up, fists clinched and teeth gritted. "Why is he being such a jerk? I don't know why I believed him, he hasn't changed at all!" She turned and noticed Jeff's proximity. "Uh ... sorry." Her cheeks reddened.

Jeff chuckled. "That's okay. I don't like him either."

I sighed and put my hand on her shoulder. "What's the prob, Kiddo?"

She opened her mouth, and then shut it again.

"What?" I put my hands on my hips.

She looked back at Connor who was laughing with Gina.

"He's ... he just ... I don't want to talk about it." Ashley stormed off leaving Jeff and I staring at her back.

Alrighty then.

We let out a collective sigh and turned to study Connor. This wasn't like him. I could see him upgrading *me*, but Ashley was the best model of kid out there. I knew he loved her. I'd seen the way he looked at her.

"What is his malfunction?"

Jeff shook his head. "I'm sorry Liberty. It's always like this with her."

I don't know what you're doing, buck-o, but it better be worth it.

"No offense, Jeff, but your sister is a soul-sucking harpy."

He chuckled. "Yeah." He frowned as he watched her. "But she just saved my life."

21: Abandoned

Liberty

We made camp next to a small stream in a wooded area, a few miles past the Monroe airport. Connor slept away from Ashley and me for the first time that night, and his absence was a void we both felt. We huddled close for comfort as well as warmth.

Jeff made his bed a few yards away and Connor and Gina were both on the other side of him.

You don't want Connor. You're lucky he's showing his true colors now.

I repeated the words in my head so many times I almost believed them. Finally the soft sounds of Ashley's snoring lulled me to sleep.

***June 26

It was early the next evening when we reached a quaint, little town surrounding a large body of water proudly labeled 'Lake McMurray.' A dense fog hovered over the calm, cerulean water, giving the area a mysterious and picturesque feel. The serenity of the abandoned town only highlighted the magnificence of God's creation; not to be depreciated by the near-annihilation of human life. I uselessly wished for a camera to capture the scene.

We stopped to rest our legs. Ashley and I headed for the lake, and the rest of the party went off in their own directions.

I picked up a flat stone and skipped it across the water.

Ashley watched, as the rock skipped several times, and then plopped into the deep. "How did you do that?"

"Well." I reached down and grabbed another one. "You have to find a flat rock. Like this." I held it to up. "Then you wrap your finger around the edge ... like this." She watched as I curved my index finger around the edge of the rock. "Then, you just kinda toss it with your arm to the side, like so." I released the rock in front of me and it skipped across the water, and then disappeared.

She picked up a stone and attempted to mimic my throw. Her toss was too high, and the rock went straight down into the water.

"Ugh." Ashley's shoulders drooped.

"No one gets it their first time." I handed her another stone. "You have to put more speed on it and keep it lower. You threw it too high."

She tried again, and this time the rock skipped twice.

"See, you're getting the hang of it." I handed her another one. "Try again."

Ashley glanced back toward the others. "Jeff's nice, but I still don't understand why we had to bring them. We were doing fine on our own." She threw the rock and it skipped several times. A huge grin spread across her face.

"That was awesome." I nodded toward the water. "And *I* wasn't included in the decision, remember?" I tried not to grind my teeth.

"She's gonna screw up everything. We don't need her." Ashley released another rock.

"We haven't given her much of a chance." I shrugged. "She's probably not *that* bad."

"How can you say that?" The opened mouth look she gave me made me chuckle.

"Wishful thinking?"

"And what if she starts dating my fa—my uncle?" she stopped and looked at me, like the child caught with her hand in the cookie jar.

She knows!

I raised my eyebrow and studied her long enough to intimidate the truth from a hardened criminal. It was a skill I'd learned from my mother, and she had wielded it like a sword; slashing lying children into submission. "Spill it."

"What do you mean?" She flashed me a crooked smile.

I winced. "You don't think I'm stupid, do you?"

Ashley shook her head.

"Start talking. What do you know?"

She let out a dramatically deep breath. "Everything."

I nodded and held her gaze until she continued.

"Mom let it slip last year. She told me that when I'm being impossible my eyes look just like my father's. Well, dad has blue eyes that never looked like mine. So I bugged Mom until she told me everything. She made me promise not to tell them—said it would destroy daddy and scare the heck out of Connor."

I nodded. "Sound advice. Your mom must have been a pretty great person."

"Yeah, you would have liked her." Her arms wrapped around herself. "I miss her so much."

I walked over and gave Ashley a sideways hug. "I'm sure she's up there—" I glanced toward the sky, "—watching over you."

Ashley's eyes started misting over. She wiped away the evidence and stared at me. "Really?"

"Of course. If I left a child with Connor, I'd never be able to sleep." I messed up her hair. "Your mom is probably so worried, she's watching you constantly."

The conversation between Ashley and I was cut short by the return of our three traveling companions. Jeff came and skipped rocks with Ashley and me, while Connor and Gina continued their conversation apart from the group.

I was handing Ashley another rock when Jeff eyed the markings on my left wrist.

"What happened?"

I turned my arm over and pushed up the sleeve of my shirt, exposing the letters.

"WWL?" He cocked his head to the side.

"Watch, wait and listen." I frowned at my wrist, and then sat down. Ashley and Jeff followed my lead.

"I was in Centralia heading for Olympia to find my sister. It was early evening and I came across a woman who was crying on the porch of a house. I didn't really pay attention to my surroundings, and approached her, thinking I'd found a friend, and maybe we could help each other." I paused, remembering the girl. "She was thin and short; about twenty, with long, dark hair. Her shoulders shook as she sobbed." I stared at the birds swooping down into the water, not wanting to relay my story, but feeling like it was somehow important.

"When I approached her, she grabbed my wrists and held me as a man attacked me from behind. He knocked me out cold. When I awoke, they'd taken all the food out of my pack, but for some reason left me alive." I ran my thumb over the carved letters. "I cut myself out of anger and frustration at my stupid mistake. I should have been paying attention—should have recognized the trap." I shrugged. "I make stupid mistakes when I'm impatient."

Jeff studied my wrist for a moment, and then ran his index finger over it. The sensation was odd; not creepy, just uncomfortable.

I slowly pulled my wrist away and placed my palm on the ground. "I guess I did it to remind myself of what I needed to change."

His expression was skeptical. "You can't change the fact that you make mistakes."

I smiled at him. "Unfortunately. But the letters remind me that I need to think—to watch, wait, and listen—*before* I act."

"Hmm." His brows bunched together and he stared at the water for a minute.

I pushed his shoulder playfully. "Hm? What's that about? Don't tell me there isn't anything you'd change about yourself."

Sad, blue eyes searched my face, and then turned toward his sister and Connor.

"Everyone screws up." I put my hand on his shoulder, forcing his attention back onto me. "You don't know me, but I'm not exactly a saint." I attempted a smile. "If my momma knew half the stuff I did, she'd tan my hide."

The side of his mouth turned up, and then his eyes locked on mine.

Broken. Hurting. Oh God, he's so lost.

My eyes were drying out, but I refused to blink.

"Jeff, I need you!" Gina's shrill demand broke the trance.

My hand slipped off his shoulder as he leaned toward me, adjusting his feet to stand.

"You can't change *who* you are," he whispered before he walked away.

We biked north on Highway 9 for a few more miles, until we found a safe spot to set up camp. Connor unrolled Princess Gina's sleeping bag as her highness made doe eyes at him.

Ashley huffed, grabbed my wrist, and led me away from the camp. When we were out of earshot from the others she started talking.

"You're really going to sit back and watch this?" She gestured toward the rest of our party.

"What?" I shrugged. "Connor and Gina? Their relationship isn't any of my business." I glanced over my shoulder in time to see Gina scoot closer to Connor. "What do you think I should do?" I stared into her dark, naive eyes. I didn't like Gina either, but it wasn't like I had any claim on Connor. Not like I even *wanted* a claim on the man.

Oh crap.

I did a mental head-palm. "Oh. *Oh*, Ash. You're still trying to play matchmaker, aren't you?" I sighed.

"I wish things were that easy, kiddo, but unfortunately they never are." I sat down, gesturing for her to do the same. "Connor will make his own decisions. He'll be with whoever he wants." An unsettling mental picture of his arms wrapped around Gina popped into my head. I placed my hands on the grounds and braced myself to keep from shuddering.

Ashley pouted. "He doesn't *really* like Gina."

I raised an eyebrow. "He told you this?"

"Not exactly." She shrugged.

"Ash, what *exactly* did he say?"

She fidgeted, pulling the leaves off the bush she stood next to. "Well we haven't actually spoken since we picked them up, but I know that's how he feels."

I took a deep breath and wondered if my own childhood observations had been so implausibly sightless. All of the air rushed out of my chest with a huff. "Ashley, what do you want me to do?"

"I want you to fight for him. You're so much better for him than she is. He can't possibly like her."

"Fight for him?" I chuckled. "And what would I do with him if I won? In case you haven't noticed, all the planets must be in perfect alignment before Connor and I can even manage a full conversation without yelling at each other. We're just not good for one another."

She clenched her stubborn jaw. "Mom said relationships are hard. You have to work at them."

My chest tightened. I wanted to make her happy. She had a rough life and she didn't ask for much, but this order was beyond my ability to fill. Even if I was interested in him—which I *almost* definitely wasn't—he no longer even acknowledged my existence.

"He hasn't even looked my direction since Gina showed up." I shrugged. "I'm not what he wants. And you know what? I'm glad we ran into her. It gave me a chance to see the type of woman Connor is attracted to. And it's not me, Ash."

She sighed. "He asked me to help him get to know you. He said he wanted to spend time with you." Her eyes glistened. "Why would he say those things if he didn't mean them?"

I sympathized with the depth of her dream and hoped it wasn't too painful when she woke up. I draped my arm over her shoulder.

"We won't ever work out. Connor will always be Connor, and I will always be me."

Ashley quickly found sleep that night, but it evaded me for hours. Connor and Gina wanted privacy and slept well away from us. I couldn't escape the betrayal I felt. He'd cast his own daughter aside just as easily as he had me. Ashley's eyes cried out in pain while her lips defended the man hurting her.

Why would You take her parents and leave her with ... this? Hasn't she suffered enough? Where are You?

I couldn't feel anything. I hadn't heard the *call* in a long time and I missed His presence.

Did I do something wrong?

Have I been abandoned by You too?

I stared at the sky, praying for answers, but none came.

"You still awake?" Jeff whispered, interrupting my silent questions.

"Yeah." I shifted in my bag. "Can't sleep."

"Me either." He rolled closer.

I smiled; thankful for the companionship. "What's on your mind?"

"Um ... Regrets." His voice sounded stoic.

"Regrets? You're so young. What could you possibly regret?"

"You're not that much older than me." Jeff sounded offended. "And lots of things. Don't you have any regrets?"

I thought for a minute. Listening to the faint hum of the other conversation, I gritted my teeth. "I've made lots of mistakes, but I don't know that I regret any of them. They've all helped me somehow. And thankfully God doesn't require my perfection."

Jeff shifted. "You believe in God?"

"Do you really think *we* are the most advanced beings in the world?" I asked. "We couldn't even save our country. I refuse to believe that there is nothing more powerful than *us*."

He chuckled. "I see your point."

"Besides." I turned on my side and propped myself up on my elbow to face him. "I've seen too much to not believe in God."

"Really?" His tone sounded interested.

"Yeah. Like the summer I turned fifteen—I was at church camp, swimming with a group of friends. The boy I had a crush on dove into the water and hit his index finger on the bottom of the pool. It instantly swelled and turned purple. He all but cried over the pain as I walked with him to the nurse's station, where the nurse diagnosed his finger as broken. She set the bone, put one of those metal thingies on it to stabilize it, and then wrapped it up good."

"Uh-huh."

The moon provided enough light that I could see Jeff watching my lips move as I spoke. I smiled. He was so unlike Connor, whose gaze was usually a few inches lower.

"Well that night at chapel we prayed for him, and I can't explain it, but I *felt* something happen. He unwrapped the bandage and bent his finger moving it all over the place. It wasn't swollen or even discolored anymore."

Jeff's brows knit together as he processed my story. He opened and closed his mouth a few times before words actually escaped. "That's ... unbelievable." His tone was skeptical.

I nodded. "Indeed. But I was with him. I know he broke his finger. I'm not crazy, and I didn't *want* to believe it either. But how do you deny something that's right in front of you?"

Jeff was quiet for a while. He rolled onto his back and stared up at the sky. "The kid was a good guy right?"

"What?"

"I mean that sort of stuff only happens to good people." He zipped his sleeping bag closed.

I laughed. "What is a good person? None of us are worthy. We're all imperfect and human. But it's not about us or what we've done. It's about grace." I let out a deep breath. "I've done some pretty bad things in my life, but I've been forgiven. No one is beyond His pardon."

"Grace." It sounded like Jeff was trying the word out; swishing it around his taste buds to check the vintage. It was the last thing he said that night. We both drifted off sometime shortly after.

When I awoke the next morning everyone but Ashley was gone.

Carved into the ground under where Jeff's sleeping bag had been were two words: Forgive me.

22: Mourning

Liberty

***June 27

Why would he— Where did they—
My head swam with incomplete thoughts.
Oh Ash.
I stared at Connor's sleeping daughter.
His daughter. How could he leave his own daughter?
Tears started to cloud my eyes, but I willed them away.
I will not cry over that selfish, heartless, arrogant ...
The thought of delivering the words that would bring Ashley more pain made me sick to my stomach.
Wish he'd been man enough to tell her himself!
God? You there? I could really use some help here.
The *call* remained silent. But that was normal. I'd gone almost a year in high school without feeling it. It was irritating, but typical not to hear from Him for extended periods of time. Answerless, I broadened my shoulders and woke up the little girl.

"What's wrong?" Ashley asked the minute she saw my face.

I sighed. "Connor, Gina, and Jeff are gone."

"What do you mean, gone?" She stood and looked around. "Gone where?"

"Just gone." I hunched my shoulders, feeling defeated. "All we have is this." I pointed toward the message Jeff left us.

"Forgive him? He's not even here to forgive! What about Connor?" She ran to the area where he had slept. "He didn't leave a message?"

"I'm sorry." The tears I kept denying battled me for the right to fall. "If he left us a clue, I can't find it."

Ashley searched the area again and again. I watched her, reminded of all the times I'd searched through my purse looking for the car keys I knew were locked in my house.

At least she still has hope.

"He wouldn't— He can't—" Her small frame shook with anger. "He promised!"

I bit down on my tongue until it bled, but it didn't stop the tears from falling. "I'm sorry."

If Connor was standing before me now, I would shoot him without hesitation.

"He wouldn't do this!"

I started rolling up my sleeping bag—nothing to do now, but keep moving forward. Our abandoners had escaped with the food bag, but I couldn't bring myself to divulge that information.

Can I pick a man, or what?

"He'll be back. I know he will." Ashley paced while I packed. "We can't just leave. We have to wait for him."

"He's not coming back." I rolled up her sleeping bag. "We *need* to get to Canada."

"No." She crossed her arms and stuck out her stubborn jaw. "I won't leave without him."

Hope can be an extremely unhelpful personality trait.

I shoved Ashley's sleeping bag into her pack and handed it to her. She didn't take it, so I set it on the ground.

"I know you're hurting, but we can't stay here. I'm leaving, and if you want, you're more than welcome to join me." I started walking toward my bike.

Please don't call my bluff.

My heart lightened when I heard the pitter-patter of her feet behind me.

We continued north on Highway 9 until we reached an extremely big lake unimaginatively named *Big Lake*. The day was warming up, but Ashley was not. The only noises that came from her direction were made by her bike. I was the one who remained, so I was the unfortunate recipient of her anger.

Annoyed by her silent treatment, I let out a deep breath. "Look," I stopped my bike and faced her. "I'm doing the best I can. I'm angry too. I'm confused and disappointed and ... and all the things that you're feeling right now. I feel them too. I don't know why he left us. I can't make him come back. I'm sorry, Ash. If he was here now, I would kick his butt for making you feel this way. But he's not here. So what do you want me to do?"

Tears rolled down her face. "I'm sorry, Libby. I know ... I just ..."

I laid down my bike, walked over, and held her as she sobbed.

"I could have gotten to like her. I would have tried." Her words were spoken between hiccups.

"No." I squeezed her. "This is not about you. And we don't know for sure. They may have taken him."

Yeah right. Mrs. Perfect and Jeff ...

I winced. I liked Jeff.

I comforted Ashley as she cried on my shoulder. "We'll be okay, I promise." I patted her back. "I'm not going anywhere without you."

We had been back on the bikes for a while when she finally spoke again.

"What's Canada like?"

I shrugged. "I've never actually been there, but Michelle has been living in Kamloops for about five years now. She said it's a lot drier than western Washington. The winter is shorter and the summer is longer. In the pictures she sent me, it looks a lot like my hometown in south-central Oregon; sagebrush, mountains, and juniper."

Ashley's look of interest encouraged me to continue. "It's a large city, about 100,000 people."

"That's like twice the size of Olympia." Her eyes grew round.

"Yeah, it's pretty big." I raised my eyebrow at her. "You know, you're going to have to work on a few things."

"Hm?" She messed with the handlebar of her bike.

"Well, you're gonna have to start saying *'eh'* after every sentence and pronouncing about as *'ahboat'*."

She looked at me sideways, and I could almost see the wheels spinning in her head.

"That right, *eh*? *Ahboat* time I start—" An eruption of giggles impeded her progress.

"*Mahvelous dahling.*" I made some goofy, grand gesture with my hand. "You'll pass for a Canuck yet."

I heard a thud and glanced in her direction—Ashley toppled from her bike.

"Ash!"

There was a sharp pain in the back of my neck.

Darkness overcame me.

23: Decision

Connor

She made me sick.

Everything about her disgusted me, from her fake smile to her annoying laugh. I hated the way she looked down her nose at Ashley and Liberty. I detested her overpowering perfume. I loathed the decision she forced me to make.

***June 25

I knew we were being followed, but dismissed the feeling as paranoia since there was no evidence. Absolutely none—until I heard the twig snap behind Ashley. I looked toward the bush and saw movement. I could have followed our stalkers then, but it would have been foolish to leave Liberty and Ashley alone and unprotected.

When Gina and Jeff appeared—siblings waiting for their dad—I knew we were in trouble. I wasn't stupid, and their story had too many holes. There were no bags under their eyes; no signs of malnutrition. They had to be something more than what they said.

Jeff projected anger, defiance, and insecurity in equal proportions. I'd place him in his early twenties with Gina about ten years older. She definitely did not have a problem with her confidence. Every move she made appeared to be calculated; like a performer, comfortable in front of her audience.

So who are they and what do they want?

Over the years I've faced multiple unknown adversaries and learned that it's always best to play along until you can sufficiently assess the threat. So, I did exactly what Gina would expect. I turned up the charisma and fine tuned my game. After all, I wasn't after her body; just her trust.

She reached for one of the ducks I carried.

"Nope." I slid away from her. You're far too beautiful to be carrying around dead birds."

The smile she flashed me was an invitation.

Maybe it would be more beneficial to tackle her body and *her trust.*

I carried the ducks to a small clearing a few yards off the road. Ashley removed the pan from her backpack and held it toward me, glaring all the while. I left her standing there as I gathered sticks and started a fire.

"She is so ridiculously uncoordinated," Gina muttered with her arms crossed. Her lip raised in contempt as she watched the scene on the road.

I followed her gaze. Jeff had one arm wrapped around Liberty with the other on her bike, trying to keep her from falling.

He could help without *fondling her.*

I gritted my teeth and glanced at Ashley. She was glaring at the back of Gina's head; fists clenched, jaw set. My reply ran through my head.

Painful, but necessary.

I had to get into Gina's mind and find out who she was and what she wanted.

Gina turned toward me and I rolled my eyes at Jeff and Liberty.

I swallowed. "Yeah, some people will stop at nothing to get attention. Of course then there are women like you, whose very presence demands appreciation."

Damn, I'm good.

Gina flashed me a conspiratorial grin. There was a loud thud as Ashley dropped the frying pan and ran off—back toward Jeff and Liberty.

Sorry kid. But I have to protect you.

I swallowed the lump in my throat as Ashley stared back at me from the road with her broken heart in her eyes.

"So you can cook?" Gina's question reminded me of what I was supposed to be doing. I nodded and picked up the pan. The desire to bash Gina over the head with it brought a smile to my lips.

Not yet. Know your enemy before you strike.

***June 26

The second night I slept beside Gina made my skin crawl.

What's wrong with me? She's gorgeous and she obviously wants me.

She felt ... wrong; almost as wrong as it felt to watch Jeff scoot his sleeping bag closer to Liberty. I tried not to scowl as Liberty turned toward him and they started talking.

Gina giggled. "You don't have to worry about my brother. He's not man enough to do anything. Of course *why* would you be worried?"

My eye started twitching. I knuckled it, grateful for the darkness. "Why indeed?"

Her giggles continued as she went into another pointless story about shoes, or clothes, or her now non-existent job, and dead friends, while I pleaded for my ear drums to burst. I glanced at the others. We were too far away to be sure, but they appeared to have fallen asleep.

Lucky.

"What I wouldn't give for a good Pinot Grigio." Gina's voice had a suggestive edge to it.

Ah wine! Finally something I care about.

I smiled back at her and hoped I hadn't missed anything important during the conversational black out.

"And what would you do with a good bottle of Pinot?"

This time her giggle sounded remarkably like a cackle as she threw her head back and stuck out her chest. "Cast away all inhibitions, live for the moment, and do whatever I want."

"Oh really?" I leaned closer.

"Yeah," she purred. "Pity we don't have any."

She's beautiful and she can't resist me. Why is this difficult?

"You know, two consenting adults don't necessarily need alcohol to raise their temperatures."

"Really?" She licked her lips.

I nodded. "They just need to relax and allow their bodies to do the thinking for their prohibitively exhausted brains."

She leaned toward me and whispered into my ear, "Show me."

Right, wrong and indifferent be damned. I closed my eyes as my lips found their way to hers. We kissed: thin lips, zero chemistry, and wrong scent. The experience was like expecting a Red Ryder BB gun, but finding a lump of coal under the Christmas tree instead. Confirmation came when I opened my eyes and found Gina—instead of Liberty—staring back at me. Disappointment descended; darkness could not fool my senses.

Leaves rustled in the bushes beside us.

"What the—" I grabbed my glock and jumped to my feet, aiming in the direction of the noise. "Stay down, Gina."

She stood, placing a hand on my gun arm. "Connor, it's okay, just don't be stupid. There are dozens of them."

Comprehension froze the blood in my veins as I turned and gaped at her. "You—"

"It's okay. Just give me the gun and no one will get hurt." She held out her hand expectantly.

She's unarmed.

My eyes swept the perimeter of the camp. Thick bushes, trees; they could be hiding anywhere.

Dozens?

Three shadows emerged from the bushes with weapons aimed at me.

I stared at Gina, seething with anger.

She played me?

Gina rubbed her hand soothingly down my arm. "I'm sorry it had to be like this. It doesn't change anything between us."

My jaw dropped. "Between us? You just—"

Her hand stilled on my arm and her voice hardened. "Think Connor. You're not the only one who will die." She glanced toward the girls.

How could I be so stupid?

24: Welcome

Connor

***Southwestern border of Mount Baker National Forest, Washington, June 26

Commander Ortega studied the cave before him. It was large and easily defendable with a small stream flowing beside it.

He crossed himself and bowed his head. "Thank you, Father—your blessings are plentiful."

A Soldier approached and saluted, waiting to be acknowledged.

"Niehls." The Commander nodded at his man. "Report."

"Sir, we've located their base—six miles due west."

The Commander's eyes widened. "God is good." He kissed the crucifix that hung around his neck. "Did anyone get close enough to get a head count?"

"Yessir. It's gonna be rough."

"Come then. Let's call a counsel. No time to waste."

***

In the darkness all I could make out was the outlines of the men heading my direction.

Gina leaned over and whispered into my ear. "Just come with us. Be easy and no one will get hurt."

"What about them?" I nodded toward the girls.

"Up to you." She shrugged. "They can come, or we can leave them behind." She nibbled on my ear and I pushed her away.

"They stay. And I swear, if anything happens to them—"

"You can't hold that against me. I'm not responsible for them if they stay behind."

Gina held all the cards. I wasn't about to drag the girls along into God-knows-what. They'd be better off on their own. And maybe if I played nice she wouldn't harm them.

"They stay." I held the handle of my gun toward her. "I'll do whatever; just leave them out of it."

"I knew you'd see reason." Her voice dripped with satisfaction as she took the gun from me.

"Wow." Jeff's body language was hostile as he stood before me. "You're leaving behind a woman and child to fend for themselves? You're a real piece of work, Dunstan."

You have no idea kid.

Gina's face distorted as she turned on her brother. "You shut your mouth. You know nothing! And if you wake them up, you can stay here with them. Permanently." She ejected the clip from my gun, studied its contents, and snapped it back in.

Jeff's shoulders drooped. "Gina—"

"Ugh, you're so weak. You shouldn't even be along for this. Why don't you go ... counsel someone?" She stormed off into the bushes.

Jeff glared at me for a moment before he crept back over to pack up his belongings.

The three Soldiers watched as I rolled up my sleeping bag and put my pack over my shoulders.

Gina reappeared and grabbed her things. "Let's go." She turned toward the road and started walking.

Jeff glanced back at the girls, glared at me, and shook his head.

The moon was in the middle of the sky as Ashley and Liberty slept through our departure. It all seemed so unreal, like there should be some sappy goodbye, tears, or something.

They're gonna be so pissed.

I'd promised Jacob I would take care of Ashley. As I silently and unceremoniously said goodbye, I wondered if my brother would have made the same choice. The only way I could keep the promise I'd made to him was to walk out on it.

If I thought about that enough, I'd go crazy.

More shadows joined us once we reached the road, bringing the armed escort count up to six.

"Search him." The order came from a voice sounding barely past puberty to the left of me.

Someone grabbed the pack from my shoulders while another started patting down my person. I had a knife in a holster around my waist and another strapped to my ankle; the searcher found and removed both. The person behind me kept my pack and we started on our way.

I leaned close to Gina and quietly whispered, "Who are these people and where are they taking us?"

"My father's Soldiers. They're taking us to him." She searched the group. "Where's Jeff?"

"Your father?" I shook my head. "You said you didn't know where *your father* was."

She shrugged. "Yeah, well?" She glanced behind her. "He better be here."

"Soldiers?" The man who frisked me had been wearing fatigues, but Soldiers? The voice issuing the order sounded so young.

Soldiers of what?

"So ... military?" I felt a twinge of hope.

Is the military reorganizing?

"Not exactly." She sighed. "Jeff! Dammit where is he?" She pointed at one of the Soldiers. "You."

The man nodded. "Yes ma'am."

"Find my brother. Shoot him if he's not with the company."

"Yes ma'am." The Soldier saluted and started to turn away.

Jeff appeared and put an arm around Gina. "Aw, shucks, Sis. I didn't know you cared."

She elbowed him in the side and he pulled his arm away, covering his stomach.

"Can't have you running off to help the wounded animals. You know Daddy wouldn't approve."

Jeff gritted his teeth. "Oh no." He covered his mouth with his hand in mock horror. "Anything but the old drunk's displeasure."

Gina slapped him. I heard the impact before I realized what had happened. He stood with his hands to his sides, seething.

"You're an ungrateful little whelp. That 'old drunk' is our father and he's doing more to help this country than anyone else. He deserves your loyalty."

Jeff held her glare for almost a full minute before his shoulders slumped in defeat. "I'm here aren't I?"

Jeff's shadow faded into the background as he stopped walking to fall behind. Gina watched him, and when he took a step forward she returned her attention to me.

"What do you mean, not exactly?" I asked, dreading the information I anticipated.

"Hm?" She turned toward me.

"How is your father not exactly military?"

"Oh." She glanced at the men around her. "These guys weren't military. They were part of the Progression."

My breath caught.

Oh hell.

The progression definitely wasn't military. They were more like a lab experiment gone horribly wrong. Only the test subjects were young adults whose service earned them side effects much worse than cancer. In an attempt to better supply our nation's military with fully prepared Soldiers, we had armed children.

Headed by Lieutenant Donovan Justice, the program started as MTCT or Military Training Camps for Teens. The goal was to provide young adults with a better understanding of military life and patriotism. Initially, MTCT focused exclusively on preliminary training; obstacle courses, marches, first-aid, navigations, communications, and team building. The children excelled at the menial tasks, encouraging their leaders to advance them to hand-to-hand combat. Artillery training was the natural next step.

MTCT began months before I left the army. By the time I began practicing law, Lieutenant Justice had transformed the program into a controversial branch of the military called the Progression. Arguments ensued about giving children—who didn't fully understand the value of life—the ability to end lives. After a long, expensive, political battle, the military was granted the freedom to arm their guinea pigs. The pliable and easily swayed children were taught a whole new level of dedication and the government had a terrifying, new tool.

The sun was coming up when we reached Big Lake. We turned down a side street and kept going when the road ended, following a man-made trail away from civilization. We crossed streams and ducked under branches, continuing on the trail until early afternoon.

I knew we were getting closer by the sudden increase in patrols. Men marched in twos, loaded with weapons, calling out challenges and replies. A waist-high barbed wire fence surrounded the base, woven around the trees to discourage anyone from coming or going except by the main entrance. The camp consisted of six large tents and numerous smaller ones, running along a small stream.

"Welcome home." Gina spread her perfect lips over her perfect teeth in another perfectly plastic smile.

Making me perfectly nauseous.

I pasted an equally artificial smile on my own face. "It looks ... efficient."

They led me around the fence, through the main entrance, and toward a large tent at the center of the camp. Conversations buzzed around me, but the loudest voice came from inside the tent. One of my guards slipped inside, and a few minutes later I was invited in to meet the Major.

He laughed as I entered.

"This *is* a treat." The voice of the Major boomed, still thick with unsuppressed delight. "Hello Commander Dunstan. Welcome to my camp." He held out his hand.

This was the man who gave Gina her arctic, calculating eyes. His russet colored hair was short and thinning, framing a face made up of hard angles and sunken features. His breath reeked of whiskey and his eyes glowed with the tell-tale signs of insanity. The man's barely five and half foot frame emphasized his stocky build, and when he moved, he did so with a limp.

"No one has called me that in quite some time." I stared at the hand held out to me, and then glanced around the tent. Eight Soldiers glared at me, so I reached out and grasped the Major's hand firmly. "I'm just an attorney now, or haven't you heard, Major ... I'm sorry sir, but you seem to have me at a disadvantage?"

The man chuckled again. "Major Jack Thompson. I trust my daughter took good care of you?" He gestured toward Gina.

"Yes, Daddy." Gina sauntered over to the Major and kissed his cheek.

"Gina." He scooped his daughter up into a hug, and then held her at an arm's length, examining her appearance. "You look tired.

"I am fatigued. It'll be nice to be back on a cot tonight."

The Major readdressed me. "I'm afraid I've spoiled her." He shooed his daughter away. "But it's hard not to when she looks so much like her late mother."

I smiled. "She is quite lovely."

Sure, if you're into the type of women that would kill baby seals for sport—

I turned my smile toward Gina.

—with her bare hands.

"I see you managed to bring your brother back as well." The Major looked disappointed as he nodded in Jeff's direction.

Jeff stepped forward. "Major," he said, flatly.

"You were lucky this time; Gina came for you. If you leave this camp without permission again, I will come myself." He sneered at his son. "And you will not be so lucky."

"Yes Major." Jeff lowered his eyes and stepped back into the shadows.

Another young Soldier entered the tent, and stood to attention.

"Ah, Rohjers." The Major smiled at his man. "Report."

"They're here, Sir." The newcomer kept his pose, awaiting further orders.

"Well what are you waiting for?" A sadistic grin spread across the Major's face as he watched my expression. "Send the ladies in."

25: Captured

Liberty

My eyes felt like they were glued shut.

Clip clop, clip clop, clip clop.

The sound was obnoxiously loud, and my head beat in time with it.

Clip clop, clip clop, clip clop.

The scent was familiar: leather, sweat and ... and ... horse?

I tried again to open my eyes.

Darkness.

Maybe they are open and it's night?

No, there would be shapes or something.

Am I blind?

I searched my memory for clues. There had been bikes, and Ashley fell ...

Ashley?

I tried to move my hands to feel around for her, but they were as uncooperative as my eyes, and continued to dangle.

Dangle? I'm upside down?

My hands were definitely above my cotton-stuffed head. I swallowed, trying to push any available saliva down my sandpaper-coated throat. Something dug into my chest, making it difficult to breathe.

One eye finally opened, and then the other.

The undercarriage of the horse greeted me, complete with a dirty-grey cinch. The ground passed by; above my head.

My face itched, but I couldn't convince the muscles in my arm to bend properly so I could scratch it. I leaned forward, hoping to rub it on the horse's stomach. It took forever to get my body to cooperate, and once it finally moved, I couldn't get it to stop.

Clip clop, clip, clop, swish, thud.

"Ouch."

Yay! I spoke.

The sun was in the center of the sky, now directly in front of me. I was lying on the ground, in the middle of a well trodden dirt path in the forest. Trees loomed all around me. The horse I'd been riding stopped, turning to look at me like I was the most idiotic human she'd ever carried. After all, my job hadn't been very difficult. She was the one doing all the work.

Shadows moved in and pulled me to my wobbly feet.

"Steady, there." A teen boy stood before me, speaking encouragement.

"Is she okay?" The voice came from behind me.

"I don't know, how much did you use?" The boy ahead of me spoke again.

"No more than normal, but look at her. When did she eat last?"

When did I eat last? We didn't eat breakfast. Last night?

The rapid changes in elevation, the insatiable pounding of my head, the ping-pong match of conversation, and finally the idea of food did me in. I leaned over and tried to throw up.

My hands were braced on my knees, as I struggled to regain control of my stomach. The fire in my throat burned hotter with each dry heave.

"Water. Please." I asked the question of no one in particular, holding out my hand expectantly.

Staring at my feet, I heard rustling, footsteps, and then felt the weight of the water bottle in my hand. I put it to my lips.

Stupid cap.

I fumbled with the cap until someone grabbed it out of my hands and returned the bottle opened. I filled my mouth, swished a few times, and spit. Then I drained the rest of the bottle. The first few gulps were torturous, but once the sandpaper in my throat became lubricated, the water felt like Neosporin. The good kind—with pain reliever.

I took a deep breath. "Thank you." Someone took the bottle from me, led me back to the horse, helped me mount, and adjusted the stirrups.

"Thanks." I positioned myself comfortably and released the stranger's hand.

Something was missing. "Ashley?"

He pointed toward the horse that Ashley's form was slung over. "She's fine. Just sleeping."

The stranger climbed back on his horse and we all started moving. The man in front of me held my reins. Four young men surrounded us. I had no idea who they were or where they'd come from. The last thing I remembered was—

"Where are our bikes?" My tongue seemed swollen, causing my words to slur.

What is wrong with me? I sound like an idiot.

I feel like an idiot.

The boy closest to me gave me a very perplexed look.

Wrong question?

Surrounding us? An escort?

"Where are you taking us?"

The boy continued to stare at me. "The Major will answer your questions."

"Major? Who are you?" Everything seemed so foggy. I rubbed my eyes and tried to focus.

Clip clop, clip clop, clip clop.

The horse's footsteps were my only response.

"Please." My voice sounded desperate. "I don't understand."

"We are not allowed to converse with prisoners." A voice behind me replied, also sounding young. I widened my eyes and looked at my escort. The boy beside me had a pimply face and long, gangly arms—maybe sixteen—if even that. I glanced at the others; none of them looked old enough to be out of high school.

Maybe Peter Pan is their Major?

I scratched my head. "Prisoners?"

The youth riding ahead of me turned in his saddle. Dark eyes glared at me under brown, unruly eyebrows. "Yes. Now shut up, or we'll have to shut you up." His lip curled up in a sneer.

It was amazing how fast the tips of my horse's ears became fascinating.

A little help here?

The mysterious horsemen led us into a large camp, bustling with activity. It looked like an anthill where all the insects wore camo and carried guns. Each person seemed to be going out of their way not to look at me, and I wondered just how much trouble I was in.

The place smelled of campfires, food, and too many people too close together with no indoor plumbing. I hoped we wouldn't be staying long, and questioned whether or not Ashley and I would live through the visit.

We rode to a large tent in the center of the camp. One of the men unloaded Ashley, draping her sleeping form over his shoulder. I dismounted, and another man grabbed my wrist. Someone motioned for us to enter.

The flap closed behind us, and it took a moment for my eyes to adjust to the change in lighting. I closed them to help the process along. When they opened, the first thing I saw was Connor. He leaned against a table beside Gina. She saw my gaze and slid closer to him.

Connor wasn't bound, gagged, or forced against his will. In fact he looked like he was eating something.

A ... guest?

"You!" I shouted as I broke free from my captor's loose hold and lunged at the man who'd abandoned us. The tent erupted in chaos, but I saw and heard none of it. My mind focused on the memory of the pain in Ashley's eyes when she awoke to discover Connor's betrayal. Her voice played through my mind, reminding me of how she defended the pig who'd abandoned her. I wanted his blood.

I reached behind me for my gun, but it wasn't in my waistband.

Pity.

It didn't matter. I could still strangle him. My hands were just closing around his neck when the Soldiers reached me. It took three men to pull me off Connor. I struggled—kicking, shouting, and throwing punches—determined to get free.

"How could you?" I was inches from him, and tears of anger and frustration streamed from my eyes. My captors held my hands firmly behind my back. "I trusted you! She trusted you!" I squirmed, ignoring the painful pull on my shoulders.

Loud, eerie laughter shook the tent; one part mirth, two parts malicious, two parts creepy. The type of laugh you'd hear from a mad scientist right before he revealed his evil plan to take over the world.

My shoulders stooped as Connor's betrayal sunk in.

What has he done?

I glared at Connor, and his blasé expression stared back at me.

Stupid, stupid, stupid.

You! You told me I could trust him!

My one-sided argument with God was put on hold as the man we'd amused approached us.

"Bravo." He said, applauding. He was short and thick around the waist. Thinning, brown hair with streaks of grey highlighted the many angles of his face. There was nothing intimidating about his appearance, but his laughter was a whole different story; it sent shivers down my spine.

He wiped the tears from his eyes and studied me for a moment.

"Do you always have this effect on women, Commander Dunstan?"

"As I said before, I am no longer a Commander." Connor's indifferent gaze shifted toward the Major.

"Yes, you did say that." The sinister man clasped his hands behind his back and paced. "And yet it appears that we have found your price of admission."

Little bells and whistles went off in my head, as his statement and tone tied my stomach in knots. I shook my head, hoping it would clear the alarms and grant me clarity.

"I don't believe we've been introduced, m'dear." The man held his hand out toward me. "I'm Major Jack Thompson."

I looked at his hand, and then glanced at my arms which were being held tight by his goons.

The Major chuckled. "It's alright boys. She promises to play nice now. Don't you?"

Do I?

I glanced from Connor to the Major. This was a decision I was not prepared to make. Luckily, my response was unnecessary. My captors released me, and the Major grabbed my right hand and raised it to his lips.

"Liberty," I whispered. My eyes felt trapped by his. I was disgusted, terrified, and completely enthralled.

"Liberty?" What a charming name. And such a charming lady."

Charming lady? Where?

Connor stirred. "What do you want, Major Thompson?"

I pulled my hand away from the Major and watched the two men for clues about our situation.

"The Progression always has a use for talent from special forces." The Major's words threw a bone to my ravenous curiosity about Connor's past. Puzzle pieces swirled around in my head as I blindly struggled to fit them together.

"I. Am. Not. Military." Connor continued to calmly stare at the Major.

The Major dismissed him with a wave of the hand. "So you say. And I do hate to sound mellow-dramatic, but there is no revolving door here. You don't enlist, you don't leave."

Yep. Classic nut-job wannabe evil genius.

"The military shut down the Progression once before." Connor stepped forward as his body tensed and his expression darkened. "They *will* do it again."

"Oh really?" The side of the Major's mouth turned up. "Where is your military now?"

Connor dismissed the Major's question and glanced at the sleeping Ashley. "You're using human collateral to force enlistment? Do you really expect to get away with this?"

I stared at Connor and mentally scratched my head.

Forced? Human collateral?

I glanced at Ashley and felt another puzzle piece pop into place.

The Major shrugged. "We have so far. And there's no need to be judgmental. We do have very good benefits."

The way the Major eyed me made me glad my stomach was empty.

Connor opened his mouth, but the Major spoke first. "There are much worse things than dying, Commander." He looked pointedly from Ashley, to me, and then finally back to Connor.

"Lieutenant Jensen." He motioned and one of the uniforms stepped forward. "Perhaps we should find more ... comfortable accommodations for Commander Dunstan's lovely traveling companions while he considers his options."

Connor took a step forward, and Gina pulled back on his arm. She leaned into him, standing on her toes, and whispered into his ear. Her mouth stretched into a grin that reminded me of a certain green Santa, well known for stealing Christmas. As her frosty-blue eyes landed on mine fire poured into my veins.

That's it you she-Grinch, you're going down!

I mentally poured all my anger, frustration and pain into my right leg as it pushed off the ground toward Gina's grin. The force behind my roundhouse—as it connected with her jaw—was enough to jar my entire body. Gina went down hard.

I barely had time to cheer before my own lights went out.

26: Ultimatum

Connor

A snake tattoo twisted up the left forearm of the Asian man who knocked Liberty unconscious. He smiled at me and raised his arm again; preparing to throw another swing.

I'll kill him.

"That's enough boys." The Major walked over and inspected the damage his men did to Liberty.

She'd gotten in one good kick, but then the four surrounding Soldiers fell on her like a group of inmates going after a prison guard. The first swing had knocked her out, but her unconsciousness did not even slow their assault. I stood there helplessly as the Major showed me his teeth; daring me to intervene.

"I like this one, Commander. She's feisty." The Major smiled at Liberty's unconscious form. Blood dribbled down her cheek, her lip was split, and judging by the blows I'd witnessed, she probably had a few cracked ribs. Lying on her back she seemed to struggle for each labored breath.

The Major kneeled beside Gina and gently touched her jaw, moving it from side to side. "Of course the next time she touches my daughter, she dies."

I paid little attention to him, continuing to stare at Liberty's limp form.

She's okay. With that temper, I'm sure she's taken harder knocks than that.

All the pain I'd caused her and Ashley had been for nothing. They were here, and in very real danger.

Jeff emerged from the shadows and checked Liberty's vitals. He glared at me, and then gently straightened out her limbs. Sliding his hands underneath her, he lifted and cradled her form. As she hung, lifeless in his arms, he carried her from the tent, followed by two other Soldiers.

The Major followed my gaze, smiling at his son's back. "Well, well Commander. It appears my search for your currency has gained me my son's as well." He chuckled. "Most convenient." He turned back toward me. "I was beginning to wonder if he preferred his own gender."

The man holding Ashley followed Liberty's entourage. The Major signaled, and everyone filed out of the tent.

Gina spoke quietly with the medic. The Major leaned down and kissed her forehead. "You too, honey. Go get some rest."

"Connor, I—" Gina stood with the help of the medic.

I looked at her, wishing she was the one unconscious.

"You'll like it here with us ... with me." She leaned on the medic as they walked out of the tent.

The Major watched Gina leave, and then chuckled and shook his head. "You're playing with my daughter, Commander."

I stared at him and said nothing.

"No one hurts my Gina." His threat was delivered casually, but I recognized it for what it was. "Think on it. I'm sure you'll make the right choice." He smiled and headed toward the opening of the tent.

I took a deep breath. "And if I refuse?"

He turned around to face me; all pretenses of humor erased. Anger and insanity fought for control of his expression as his triumphant smile turned into a snarl.

"After what your Liberty just did to my Gina, I truly hope you do."

He left me alone in the tent, but we both knew I wasn't going anywhere. I started pacing and reminding myself of all the reasons why I couldn't accept his offer.

I cleared my throat. "I, Connor Dunstan, do solemnly swear that I will support and defend the Constitution of the

United States against all enemies, foreign and domestic; that I will bear true faith and allegiance to the same; and that I will obey the orders of the President of the United States and the orders of the officers appointed over me, according to regulations and the Uniform Code of Military Justice.

So help me God."

My parents' death had been rough on me. At sixteen, my world changed, my grades plummeted, and colleges weren't exactly knocking on my door. The military had offered me the chance to be something other than "that poor boy who lost his parents." They granted me the opportunity to become autonomous; expected to perform regardless of my past. And perform I did, scooping up all the college credits I could schedule around my training.

By the time I turned twenty, I was selected for the Green Berets. At twenty-three, I was commanding my own Operational Detachment Alpha (ODA) team.

My third year of command was brutal. I was only twenty-six when I led the botched mission in Afghanistan that took the life of two of my friends and a young boy. Once that tour ended I retired, and the government paid for the completion of my education.

Because of the recommendations of my superiors and the money the military put forth, I was able to complete my law degree at Stanford. This country had given me much, and it deserved more than my betrayal. If I joined the Progression it would be worse than treachery. I would be a tool used to further the extinction of decent human beings—a knife wielded to cut down those who opposed the savage methods of the Progression.

I couldn't accept the offer, but I couldn't decline it either. The price was too high. Liberty and Ashley would live plenty long enough to hate me for abandoning them to their fate. My death would be a coward's way out.

This is my fault. I let us get captured.

When I first suspected we were being followed, I should have turned us around.

Why didn't I?

I thought I could take care of us—that I could handle the situation. I hadn't learned from Afghanistan. I was once again overconfident, and this time the price of my arrogance increased to three lives.

No options.

My stomach clenched. I was unprepared for the way defeat affected my senses; foul-smelling, sour-tasting, putrid-feeling defeat.

One option.

No. Too terrible to even think of.

No options.

But there was always an option. I could almost see Death as it stalked me from the boarder of my consciousness. We'd had many close calls, but I'd always managed to cheat him. And now I could feel his presence like a loan shark, waiting for payment. We were living on borrowed time, but I could still control how we died.

I'll sign on with the Progression.

I gritted my teeth against the plan.

Then the first time I get the girls alone I'll kill them both, and take my own life. I won't serve the Progression, and I won't allow Liberty and Ashley to be tortured.

I could almost hear Death's laughter as I considered my one option.

"It looks like you'll get your payment yet." I closed my eyes and found my brother in the darkness.

Jacob frowned at me. "Connor, where there is death, there is also life."

I squeezed my eyes closed, welcoming the memory of Jacob at age eighteen, trying to make me understand Mom and Dad's death.

"There is no night so dark that the light can't pierce it." He messed up my hair. "I know its hard now, but it'll get better. One day you'll understand."

"No." I remembered shaking my head at his words. "I'll never understand why they had to die. You say God is all-powerful. Well why isn't he powerful enough to stop death?"

"You need to talk to Him about that." My brother faded away as I opened my eyes.

Could I kill Liberty and Ashley?

Did I have a choice?

The anger started in my toes and spread like a wild fire, feeding on the oxygen in my blood. I was defeated. I paced, and each footfall sounded harder, and more heated than the last. I clenched my fists, gritted my teeth, and turned my attention beyond the roof of the tent.

Oh yes, I'd always known God was real. It was his character I had a problem believing. Why would someone who could stop the pain choose not to? I opened and closed my mouth a few times. With so much to be angry about, I had no idea where to begin.

Every muscle in my body tensed as I directed my fury at God. "Enjoying the show? Sitting up there on your fluffy throne watching everyone suffer? You could stop this. And yet, as always, you choose to do nothing. Nothing!"

My anger grew with each word. "Are you planning on stepping in, or will you allow me to end their lives as well? Will you watch me kill everyone I love? Damn you! Intervene! Do *something*."

I collapsed, falling to my knees in the very spot where Liberty had been beaten. With my fists, I pounded on the ground until my hands split open and my blood mingled with hers. Then I raised them toward the sky. "Is this what you want? How much blood has to be spilled until you decide to climb down from your throne and get your hands dirty?"

I lowered my fists to the ground as my back slumped under the weight of my failure. "You are supposed to be all powerful; God of love, hope, forgiveness. Omnipresent, yet where the hell are you?" A tear slid down my cheek and I closed my eyes.

"Please. Help them. I would do ... anything. Be ... anything. If you would just, this one time, please ..." Tears continued to race down my face. I was so over come with emotion, I could barely speak. "I. Can't. Kill. Them."

Lost.

Desperate.

Outplayed.

I was still on my knees when I smelled the smoke.

27: Reinforcements

Connor

I inhaled deeply through my nose.

Smoke. So this is hell then?

On my knees with my eyes closed, I decided it didn't matter. "You can catch the whole damn place on fire. I'm not moving until you answer me."

Footsteps to my right preceded the current of air that flowed by, announcing that I was no longer alone.

"Then said He to Thomas," whispered the newcomer in a slight Latino accent.

My eyes burned as more tears threatened to fall at the familiarity of the voice.

"Reach hither thy finger and behold My hands."

I held my breath, wondering if I'd finally lost my mind.

It couldn't be—

"And reach hither thy hand and thrust it into My side."

I mentally tracked his speech patterns, and followed the scripture that had been quoted at me many times.

"And be not faithless, but believing."

I opened my eyes, and looked up. There was no way I could control the stupid grin that spread across my face as the man before me predictably kissed the crucifix around his neck. It was a habit I'd seen him do a million times, but this time it brought unadulterated joy to my heart.

"Boom." My voice cracked as I said the name of my old weapons specialist.

Boom looked around the tent. "So this is all it took to get you to finally seek Him?"

He hadn't changed a bit. His eyes still sparkled mischievously and his 5'6", 180 lb weapon of a body looked like it could stop a Mac truck. His dark skin was covered in a layer of dirt and gun powder. The once camouflage bandana on his head was so grimy that I could barely distinguish it from his dark hair. But all things considered, he was the most welcome sight I'd come across in years.

I knew somewhere within those fatigues, Boom was packing at least five guns, three knives, six grenades, and enough ammo to take on Arnold in a *Terminator* movie.

There was no one in the world I'd rather have at my back.

"It looks like you ran into a bit of trouble, Conman." The old nickname fell around my shoulders like a worn sweatshirt. Neither of us were as young and daring as we used to be, but being around Boom was like Ben-Gay for my soul.

"What, this?" My arms outstretched, palms up; gesturing to my overwhelming world. "I got this."

"Father forgive *mi hermano* for his lying tongue." Boom crossed himself and offered me a hand.

Outside, the chaotic sounds of gunfire and panic were getting closer.

The girls!

"I'm not alone. I was with a woman and a little girl." I took his hand and he hefted me to my feet.

"Yes, we saw them. They're being retrieved." Boom handed me a machine gun and four extra clips of ammo. The side of my mouth twitched.

He shrugged. "If you can't make it go bang it is just an expensive club."

I chuckled; glad for the confirmation that my friend remained unchanged. "You always did create the best distractions."

White teeth gleamed against his brown skin.

Boom led me out of the tent. We stepped over the bodies of my slain guards, and pushed our backs flat against structure. The air above the camp was thick with smoke as several tents burned. People carried buckets of water from the stream, and the Soldiers battled a small skirmish with what I assumed was the rest of the distraction.

A grenade appeared in Boom's hand. He pulled the ring and tossed it into a nearby tent. The side of my mouth curved up at the signal.

Just like old times.

I followed Boom to a cut section of the barbed wire fence. He motioned and we each grabbed a portion of the wire and pulled it back about a foot. Then we squeezed our way through and started inching toward the trees. A shot fired and we went prone, looking around for the shooter. I saw him just as he took aim again, but Boom's bullet hit the shooter in the left shoulder, spinning him around before he went down. My ears rang and the smell of burnt powder filled my nostrils.

The shots drew attention. A patrol group headed our direction to investigate. Another grenade appeared in Boom's hand. He pulled the ring and threw it into the group. We ducked back down as the ground shook.

Boom pointed at the trees in front of him and we crawled forward. Once under the cover of the foliage, we stood and ran. After we made it a safe distance, we slowed our pace to a fast walk.

"Where are the girls? Where's the rest of your team?" I glanced around, but saw neither allies nor enemies.

"We'll meet up at the cave."

I trusted Boom completely, but still struggled against the desire to turn around and go after my girls myself.

"How did you know I was in there?" I asked to distract my thoughts.

"We were running surveillance when they brought you in." He ducked under a branch. "I'm sure you understand my presumption that the attractive, angry-looking redhead must have been with you."

I socked Boom in the shoulder. "One time. That was one time, and how was I supposed to know she was the General's daughter?"

He smirked and stepped methodically over foliage, pushing away hanging tree limbs. Boom was the other brother I'd abandoned when I couldn't face my failure. No blood bound us, but Boom was kin in every other sense of the word. He sent me correspondence several times a year. I read every word, but never responded. And he never gave up.

"Boom—" I stopped walking, knuckled my eyes and faced him. "I ..."

"Conman." He held out his hand to me. "*Mi hermano.* Always."

I took his hand and we embraced for a two second man-hug—no more, no less—and stepped back like it never happened.

"You saw me go in?" I shook my head at him. "Took you long enough to act."

He snickered. "It is good to see you, too." His voice turned somber. "So many dead. So many worse than dead. My heart rejoices at the sight of someone I know I can trust."

We started walking again while I mulled over the limited information I had, hungering for more. I wanted details, numbers, stats, and base information.

What's going on? Who's in charge? Has there been any word from the rest of the country?

"So, the army is going after the Progression?" The familiar thirst for action stirred my blood, flaring the desire to be at the heart of tactical planning.

"You're asking me to disclose my mission to a mere civilian?" He shook his head. "You must be an imposter. The real Conman would know better."

I held up my hands. "Oh a minute ago I was your brother, and now I'm 'a mere civilian'? Where's the love?"

I could feel his eyes study me as we walked.

"Waiting to see where you stand," he replied.

"Hm?"

Boom cleared his throat. "Legend tells us of a man who was once more-than-a-man." He looked at me sideways as we continued on our way.

I rolled my eyes and settled in for another of Boom's wild stories. "Legend, eh?"

He nodded. "This more-than-a-man had the potential to achieve any position in the United States army that he desired, but instead he chose to be a Commander in the Green Berets."

"Any position?"

"Oh yes. He'd earned medals of merit, commendation, service, honor, hearts, stars ... there were so many colors on the front of his uniform that leprechauns used to show up looking for their pots of gold."

I chuckled. "Perhaps instead of Boom, we should call you Bard."

He ignored me and continued with his story. "He chose to be a Commander, because he wanted to be on the front lines with his men. He never expected any of them to do what he, himself wouldn't do."

"He sounds like an arrogant fool." I stepped around a large rock.

"But one day he discovered that his superpowers were nothing more than fable. More-than-a-man turned out to be less-than-a-superhero. Crushed by his discovered inadequacy he buried his humanity deep in the earth's core and became ... undead."

"Undead?" I laughed, shaking my head.

He nodded. "Oh yes. Only the undead would choose the path of an attorney."

My eyebrows rose as I looked at Boom.

"I've been inside a courtroom, Con. If those people aren't undead, I do not understand the meaning of the word."

"Indeed," I conceded. "So what ever happened to your friend?"

"Ah-ah-ah." He stopped walking and shook his finger at me. "It's not what happened, it's what will happen. And that I cannot tell you."

"So you made me listen to this bogus story and you're not even gonna reveal the ending?"

"Nope. You tell me. You made a promise back there." His eyes focused on mine. "Will you continue to beat yourself up over the past or will you man up and do the right thing?"

I never had to speculate about Boom's position on matters. He was always quick to divulge, even when I didn't request enlightenment.

"Man up?" I puffed out my chest. "Are you calling me a coward?"

Boom chuckled. "You are a lot of things, Conman, but never a coward."

I let my chest deflate. "How can I *man up* when I don't even know what's expected of me? How do you follow a leader who doesn't give instructions?"

He shrugged his shoulders. "Well, when I need direction I seek Him through prayer."

I shook my head at him, trying to hide my smile. "Ten years. Ten bloody years since I saw you last and you're still barking at me to pray. Come on Boom, technology, evolution, there has to be some sort of easy button or divine messaging system by now. I'd even settle for one of those collars that electrocutes me when I make the wrong decision."

He laughed. "Yes that would definitely be easier. But then it wouldn't be free will. How would we learn if not by our mistakes?"

By the time we arrived at our destination the sun was nearing its decent, cooling off the late June temperatures. Gnats and mosquitoes invaded, annoying and attacking whatever flesh was available.

The site was a large cave in the side of a hill, hidden by dense evergreens and shrubbery. Boom's team had created a single-revetted timber barricade at the mouth of the cave. It was large enough to shield about twenty Soldiers, and reinforced with earth. The north and south corners of the barricade each supported a mounted machine gun, manned by two Soldiers.

Only four men guarding?

"So few?" I asked as we neared the men.

"Fort Lewis could only spare two teams. The majority of the men should be back soon."

"Two teams?" I scratched my head. "Twenty-four men? That's all Fort Lewis could spare?"

"Our numbers are not great." Boom's expression showed his concern.

I blinked at Boom as we meandered toward the mouth of the cave. "We came from Olympia and saw very few civilians. If they didn't head for the bases where are they?"

Boom's eyes widened. "Conman, very few stayed with the army. Most went home to their families during the crisis. We had no control. But the Progression fanatics are dedicated, and the absence of monetary compensation did not discourage their loyalty." His eyes scanned the area. "And now, they're recruiting. Their enrollment procedures are very compelling."

I nodded. "Yeah, I got the whole 'join or die' proposal."

Boom watched me. "I can't believe you were not aware of this. Where have you been—in a hole somewhere?"

"No." I looked at my feet. "In a safe."

"A safe?" Boom waited for me to elaborate, but I just nodded.

Why aren't they here yet?

Anxiety wreaked havoc on my stomach, tying it in knots. "Where are my girls? What is taking your men so long?"

Boom didn't answer. Instead he picked up a canteen leaning against the barricade, took a long pull, and offered it to me. I drank and handed it back.

I followed Boom to each of the machine guns, where he introduced me to the four Soldiers; Mathers, Stein, Shortridge, and James. Salutes and reports were given while I worried about Ashley and Liberty. My mind ran through scenarios that I had no desire to accept as possibilities.

I began to pace the line of the barricade.

A loud, shrill whistle came from the trees behind us. The guards, Boom, and I all drew our weapons.

"Blue fence." Boom called out the challenge phrase.

"Sister Ann," replied a male voice from the trees.

A group of men emerged from the foliage on horseback—one of which attempted to detain a writhing, yelling Ashley.

"I said let me down!" She demanded. "If you don't tell me where Connor and Liberty are right now, I swear I will—"

"Ash," I called out as I approached. "It's okay I'm here."

"And ano—" She turned, looked down at me, and then flung herself into my arms, still sobbing.

"I told her you wouldn't walk out on us." She gripped me tightly. "Where is Libby?" She craned her head around. "No one tells me anything. They won't let me look for her. Oh and she's *sooo* mad at you."

"Isn't she with you?" I glanced from horse to horse, then man to man, but Liberty wasn't there. "Where was she the last time you saw her?"

Please say with these guys.

"Uh, we were on bikes the last time I saw her." Ashley studied the men around her. "When I woke up, that guy—" She pointed accusingly at the mounted Soldier whose horse she'd just leapt from. "—was squeezing my arms and making me sit in front of him on the horse. No one would talk to me."

My stomach sunk.

I should have gone back.

Ashley's face mirrored the anxiety I felt; eyes round, lips pinched. She grabbed my shirt and pulled my face close to her. "Where is she? You have to find her!"

I patted her on the back. "I will Ash."

Boom appeared beside me, counting his men. "Twelve? Only twelve? Where are the others?"

"They're coming, Commander," one of the men said as he dismounted. "There weren't enough horses. Those on foot left before us. They should be here soon."

Another whistle sounded from the trees.

I looked at Boom as he studied the surrounding forest.

Three short whistles followed.

Boom's jaw flexed. "Stations! We've got incoming."

Horses were pushed into the cave as Soldiers prepared to defend. A line of men knelt behind the barricade, drawing weapons, and snapping on night vision goggles.

"Get in the cave, Ash, I'll find her." I pushed Ashley behind the barricade. "I promise. We'll get through this then find her." I kneeled in front Ashley, staring into eyes identical to my own. "Ash, I need you to *stay in the cave.* Get toward the back and hide under those blankets." I pointed toward a pile of linen. "Don't come out until I come get you."

And if I don't make it?

I pointed at Boom. "See that man? He's my good friend. You can trust him if anything happens to me."

"If anything—" She shook her head, and then threw her arms around me.

I hugged Ashley, and then tapped her shoulder so she'd release me.

She pulled back and wiped away her tears, forcing a smile. "Uncle Connor." Ashley's voice shook. "I knew you'd come back. And I know you'll be fine. And we *will* find Liberty."

I smiled the little girl I never wanted, but couldn't imagine living without. "I love you Ash." I kissed her forehead and sent her into the cave to hide.

"Love you too," I heard her call over her shoulder.

28: Fight

Connor

Someone threw a vest, helmet, and night vision goggles to me. I quickly geared up and kneeled behind the barricade, close to the entrance of the cave, aiming my machine gun at the trees.

A man ran out of the bushes with his hands raised.

Boom stood and lowered his weapon. "Koyama? Report. Where are your men?"

"We were separated, Commander." The man took a step closer. "They should have been here by now."

Boom headed toward the end of the barricade, motioning for the solder to approach him. Koyama looked around nervously.

"Wait." I stood and blocked Boom.

Something felt wrong. I pulled the night vision goggles down around my neck so I could get a good look at the man.

Koyama took another step forward, and then his eyes met mine. We stared at each other. The sun was making one last, valiant effort to illuminate the sky before it gave up the day to night. It provided just enough light to reveal the snake tattoo that twisted up Koyama's forearm.

I'll kill him!

"Traitor!" I shouted.

We raised our guns simultaneously and fired off three rounds; mine at Koyama; Koyama's at Boom.

I went prone as my peripheral vision noted several white flashes lighting up the trees around us. Gunfire erupted, and the familiar smell of burnt gun powder filled the air.

Several flashes against our eighteen men caused figures and odds to float through my mind as I hit the ground beside Boom.

Boom fell with a grunt. I got to my knees and leaned over him as my hands moved quickly over his body, checking my friend for injuries. When I reached his left arm, I found the wound.

"You're hit." I leaned over him, trying to determine the damage. "Medic!"

Boom winced when I touched his shoulder. He turned his head, trying to get a look at the wound.

When the medic appeared I pulled my night vision goggles back over my eyes and resumed my position at the barricade. Koyama's body lay a few feet from the trees.

Good.

I saw another flash and fired at it. Stein kneeled beside me, shooting at his own flashes. Another of our men fell, and was being tended to further down the line.

Eventually the gunfire died down. It was impossible to know if we'd killed them all, or if they'd retreated. By the time Boom decided it was over, we had three wounded, leaving us only fifteen able bodies. Boom waited another ten minutes before ordering a sweep of the perimeter.

The sweep discovered several Progression bodies, and four that the team identified as their own, not counting Koyama.

I held my post until Boom released us, and then slid into the cave to find Ashley.

"Ash, you can come out now."

The pile of blankets wiggled, and then erupted as Ashley stood up. She ran to me and we embraced.

"I was so worried. There was all this shooting and yelling and I wanted to come out, but you said not to and it—" She wrinkled her nose. "—it really stinks in here."

I smiled and took a deep breath through my nose. "Yep. Smells like a men's locker room."

"Gross." She pushed me away half-heartedly. "Hey did you find Libby yet?"

My stomach sank. I shook my head and took Ashley's hand as we walked out of the cave toward Boom.

"I don't understand." Boom's arm had been cleaned and wrapped tight. He stood over the body of his rogue Soldier with his brows furrowed.

"He was a good kid." He shook his head. "I've known him a couple years now. Has a little sister in the Air Force, stationed in Germany. His parents were military." Boom frowned. "It doesn't make sense."

Ashley gasped when she saw the scene. I knelt, and encouraged her to hide her face in my chest. "Don't look at them. Just close your eyes."

She peeked at the fallen boys. "But they look like high school kids."

I grabbed her by the shoulders, making her look at me. "You shouldn't be here—shouldn't have to see this. Come on."

She followed me to the entrance of the cave, where we found a fallen branch to sit on. She reached down and grabbed a handful of pebbles, tossing them one-by-one back to the ground.

Someone started a campfire, and the men dug graves by the light.

Ashley stared at me with big, somber eyes. "Do you think Libby's okay?"

I pulled her close and kissed her forehead. "I hope so Ash. I miss her too."

"You do?" Ashley's eyebrows rose. "But what about *Gina*?"

I eyed her skeptically. "You didn't really believe I liked her, did you?"

"But—" The confusion on her face seemed to grow.

"Ash." I frowned. "Sometimes adults have to say and do things we don't mean."

She shook her head. "I don't un—"

"*¡Maldita sea!*" Boom's voice rang out, silencing everyone else.

I watched my friend as the light cast shadows on his face, exposing him as both ancient and ageless. His usually mischievous expression was pulled tight by agony as he stared out at his men. He removed his helmet and wiped the sweat from his brow.

"I don't understand what happened here tonight. Each one of us took vows to defend this country, against *all* enemies, foreign and domestic." He eyeballed his men. They stopped what they were doing and crowded around him.

"What's going on now?" Ashley stood and climbed onto a large rock for a better view.

"Shh. Just watch." I stood next to her and she leaned against my shoulder.

Boom cleared his throat. "Many years ago this country accepted my *madre*—allowed her to become a citizen—when she immigrated here from *México* seeking a better life for her children. To my *madre* the United States meant freedom. Freedom to work and earn enough money to feed her children. Freedom to educate my brothers and sisters, regardless of her financial shortcomings. Freedom to live and let live within the confines and boundaries of fair and honest laws." He bowed his head and crossed himself. "God rest her soul."

He stared at the corpses that lay beside half-dug graves. *"CHILDREN!"* His face distorted as he shouted the word with more vehemence than I'd ever heard him use.

I felt Ashley wince beside me. I grabbed the hand that rested on my shoulder and squeezed it.

"What sort of cowards brainwash children and send them against men?" Boom spat. "The Progression is a domestic enemy, oppressing Americans, stealing away the liberties so many Soldiers have fought—and died—to preserve."

A tear slid down Boom's cheek. "This is still God's country. And I will fight with every breath in me—every ounce of dust used to create this frail shell—to preserve it. *Hermanos* ..." His gaze encircled the crowd. "Will you fight by my side to preserve this great country?" He paused, staring at his men. "Or will you abandon your country to join the ranks of cowards, and hide behind children?"

"U. S. A." Someone chanted their response.

"U. S. A." As others joined in I felt the hair on my arms and neck stand up with excitement.

"U. S. A." Louder and louder they chanted as their voices filled the forest.

"U. S. A." Ashley and I added our voices with the others, and her face beamed with the infectious emotion of the moment.

A horse appeared in the clearing, instantly silencing the chanting. Guns cocked; Soldiers aimed.

"Identify yourself," one of our men demanded.

"Jeff Thompson," the shadow shouted back. "I'm not with your company, but I have one of your wounded."

"Liberty?" Ashley and I said the name together as we took hopeful steps toward Jeff. I held my hand up, to halt Ashley's advancement.

She eyed me angrily.

"Yeah. Requesting permission to approach. Sh—She needs medical attention."

I looked at Boom; his unit, his call.

He eyed Jeff dubiously. "Could be a trap."

"Could be," I conceded.

"Is she worth it?" He studied me, waiting for an answer.

Is she?

I looked around the half-circle of Soldiers.

Is one life worth all of theirs?

"What?" Ashley pushed her way around my outstretched hand. "Of course she's worth it. I know him, and he's a friend!" She ran toward Jeff.

"Ash, stop!" I yelled after her, but she ignored me. I gawked at the men around me as Ashley ran in front of their drawn weapons. "Boom!"

He glanced around, seeing the cause of my distress. "Lower your weapons." He ordered, gesturing to his men.

Liberty was worrisomely unconscious. The camp medic checked her pulse and nodded. He pulled up her eyelids and shined his small flashlight at her eyes. "Dilated."

Despite my objections, Ashley stood next to Jeff. She wrapped her arms around his stomach and squeezed. "I knew you were a good guy."

Jeff looked uncomfortable, rising and lowering his hands like he couldn't figure out where to put them. He ended up patting her on the head. "Uh ... thanks."

We all anxiously watched Liberty.

The medic turned toward Jeff. "How long has she been out?"

Jeff paused for a moment. "Um ... a little over four hours."

"Four hours?" The medic checked her eyes again.

"But this isn't the first time today." Jeff's winced.

We all turned toward him.

"She was hit with a tranq dart this morning. And ..." he hesitated, looking like he'd rather be anywhere but here. "She might have hit her head when she fell off the horse."

"The horse? You *dropped* her?" I took a step toward Jeff.

"Stop him," Boom commanded, nodding in my direction.

"Not me." Jeff held up his hands. "Earlier today, when they were brining her and Ashley to the camp. One of the men said she fell off the horse while she was unconscious."

The Soldier in front of me had put his hand on my chest.

I looked at Boom. "Please. Do you really think he's gonna stop me?" I nodded toward the trembling Soldier expected to restrain me.

Boom chuckled and glanced at Jeff. "Without him, she never would have made it here."

What he said made sense, but I really wanted to hit someone, and Jeff seemed like a perfectly good target. "Without *his interference*, your men probably would have found her, and she could have gotten medical attention much sooner."

"Perhaps. But what if Koyama found her?" Boom narrowed his eyes at me. "It doesn't matter. Do not touch him. That is *my* command."

Anger blended with pride as I locked eyes with Boom. The corner of my mouth twitched and he smiled. We'd had this fight before, only now the roles were reversed.

I turned my attention back to Jeff. "Why did you help her?"

"I—I don't know." He watched the medic working on Liberty. "I just ... had to. She would have done the same for me." He worried his lip as he stared at her unconscious form.

"Yeah." I nodded. "She would've." I felt my eye twitch as I watched Liberty. Acid reflux flared up and I wondered if she was giving me an ulcer.

I'm permanently attaching a helmet to her head.

The medic brought out a small vial of ammonium carbonate, uncorked it, and held the container under Liberty's nose. A hush fell over the crowd as everyone watched.

I held my breath as her eyes opened; beautiful green eyes.

She looked around the circle, casting agitated glances at the unfamiliar faces. Her brows knit together as she pushed her upper body off the ground, coming to a sitting position. She groaned and put her head in her hands.

I reached down and steadied her. "Thank God, you're okay." I released the breath I'd been holding.

Liberty turned toward me and narrowed her eyes. "You! You!" She lunged toward me. "You lying, backstabbing, abandoning, tail-chasing, lousy excuse for a human being!"

Jeff chuckled. "At least there's nothing wrong with her memory."

I glared at him and clenched my fist.

"Do you have any idea what you did to Ashley?" Liberty continued. "Do you even care? Do you—" Liberty's eyes widened. "Where *is* Ash?"

Ashley sat next to Liberty and they embraced.

The crowd disbursed as Ashley recapped her experience.

"—then Jeff showed up with you," she concluded.

Liberty smiled at Jeff, clasping his hand. "Thank you."

He blushed, nodded, and stared at the ground.

I gritted my teeth. A hand appeared on my shoulder and I glanced back to find Boom's frowning face.

"I could use some help." He gestured toward the bodies.

I nodded and followed him as he muttered his customary words of burial and prayers for the deceased.

He picked up a handful of dirt and scattered it over the dead.

Children.

My problems became insignificant as I glanced at each face of the Progression boys. Most were in their teens; several too young to shave. "So young."

"The young are easier to inspire—easier to manipulate. That's why we shut down the Progression before. Why we voted against the MTCT in the first place." Boom shook his head. "Deadly children." He crossed himself and muttered the final words. "Ashes to ashes, and dust to dust."

The tangy scent of blood faded as the bodies cooled, and the essence of life dissipated. Soon they'd be stiff with rigor mortis, followed by a rapid decay. Within weeks nothing would be left of these children but bones.

I stared down into the empty brown eyes of a slim, young boy. "There has to be a way to save them."

"Conman, they recruit. If they can't recruit, they kill." He motioned to his gun. "This is the only thing they understand."

"But maybe—" My mind raced as it suggested, disqualified, and dismissed ideas.

"No." Boom's grim face was suddenly inches from mine.

"But what about this *grace* you're always talking about? Are they not worthy of grace?"

The side of Boom's mouth turned up into a lopsided smile. "I mean no, you don't get to talk strategy, *civilian.*" He practically spat the last word. "Unless, of course, you're ready to give up on this retirement nonsense?"

I studied the young bodies stiffening before me. "To do what—kill children?"

Boom sighed. "Those beyond our help must be destroyed. They cannot be allowed to ravage this country. We must uphold the laws."

I nodded.

"But those we can help, we will." He studied me while we walked back toward the fire. "You're not the same man I knew."

I chuckled. "No. I don't know who I am anymore."

"And what about Liberty?" His white teeth reflected the fire's light. "I never thought I'd see the day a woman took down the great Conman. Bah. Legend indeed!"

I took a swing at him, but he ducked, and then winced at the pain from his arm.

I glanced at Liberty. "She hasn—"

"Yes, she has. I see the way you look at her. Even now."

"I don't know what happened." I shrugged. "One minute she wasn't worth the trouble to think about. Then the next thing I knew, I couldn't think about anything else. I was taking her and Ashley to Canada."

"Why Canada?"

"Liberty has a friend there, and was hoping that things would be different north of the border."

Boom looked at me and shook his head. "You were fleeing to Canada?" He chuckled.

I held up my hands. "Yes, but could you make it sound a little less cowardly?"

Boom's laugh quieted when his eyes landed on Jeff. "Who is he?"

"Jeff?" My eyes narrowed. "It appears he's the son of the Progression Major whose camp you just destroyed."

Boom nodded. "What's he doing here?"

Sitting entirely too close to Liberty.

"I'm not sure," I replied.

"Your Liberty," He nodded in her direction. "Do not to underestimate her role." Boom watched as Liberty and Jeff talked, and several of the younger Soldiers listened in. "She appears to have a way with the youth."

"She does, but Libby?" I watched as Liberty's smile infected those around her. "She's not military. This life isn't for her, Boom."

He considered me for a moment. "When I look at her, I can *feel* the commission on her soul." He chuckled as his gaze returned to the girls. "Liberty is called by a force so powerful not even *you* will be able to resist it."

29: Plans

Liberty

Ashley, Jeff, and I were sitting on the ground talking, when Connor approached with the man Ashley pointed out as the leader of the camp.

"Liberty." The man extended his hand to me, and as I grasped it, he hefted me to my feet. "My name is Commander Ortega, but my friends call me Boom."

His dark eyes sparkled and he seemed honest and real. I liked him instantly. "Thank you." I brushed the dirt from the seat of my pants and helped Ashley up. "My friends call me Libby."

Boom smiled. "Connor has told me much about you."

I narrowed my eyes at the slime-ball in question and he raised his hands defensively.

Boom chuckled. "No. All good, I assure you."

My eyes returned to Boom's smile. "I hear you're quite the orator, Boom."

His smile shifted toward Ashley. "Have you been telling tales on me, Ms. Ashley?"

Ashley shook her head. "No, it was Jeff. He heard you speak before he rode into the camp."

"Oh?" Boom extended his hand to my other companion. "And you—you must be Jeff."

Jeff shook Boom's hand. "Y-Yes, Commander. Jeff Thompson." He looked around, as if waiting for a reaction.

"And what's your position, Jeff? What will you choose to do?"

Jeff stared at Boom. "But my father ..."

Boom shook his head. "The son is not responsible for the actions of the father. I'm asking who *you* will become."

Jeff considered the Commander for a moment before he nodded. "My father will kill me either way."

"Best to make your life count then, isn't it?" Boom took a step back. "Walk with me, Thompson. You have proven your bravery, and I'd be honored to offer you a position on my team."

Jeff glanced at me, looking both excited and terrified.

I smiled encouragingly and squeezed his arm. "I'll be here if you need me."

As Jeff and Boom wandered away, a Soldier appeared with a sleeping bag and handed it to Connor.

"Alright, Ash. It's been a busy day. You should probably get some sleep." He handed her the sleeping bag.

Ashley hugged me, and then wrapped her arms around Connor. I stared at the girl, wondering why she'd forgiven him so quickly.

Hope he doesn't expect the same from me.

"We need to talk," Connor said as Ashley took her sleeping bag into the cave.

"No." I glared at him. "We really don't."

"Please?" Connor's eyebrows rose as he held out his hand to me.

I crossed my arms. "We don't have anything to talk about."

A group of Soldiers who were bedding down toward the front of the cave shushed us.

"Please?" Connor whispered.

I sighed. "Fine. Talk."

"Not here." He grabbed my hand and led me to the edge of the trees. Owls hooted and crickets and frogs added their voices to the night's music. A heavy moon hung in the sky as we stood on the outskirts of the fire's radius of light.

Connor turned toward me.

I pulled away and leaned against the trunk of a large evergreen. My hand roamed over the porous bark, picking at the wood.

Connor's beard had almost fully filled in, giving him a ruggedly-handsome look. I stared into his dark eyes and remembered the way he had cast me aside for Gina.

Why are the cute ones always weasels?

My hand found purchase on a large piece of bark. I tugged until it came loose from the tree, and then worried at it with my nails.

Lying, manipulative, skirt-chasing jerk.

I felt my resolve fortify around the thoughts. "You. Left. Us. What else is there to talk about?"

He continued to watch me. His top lip was barely visible under the shadows of his mustache. As he pursed his lips together, I wondered—not for the first time—what it would be like to kiss him.

Of course it would be great. He's a player; no doubt he's had lots of practice.

"You're not dumb enough to believe that." His words shattered the night's natural ambiance.

"Excuse me?" I blinked, wondering if I'd heard him correctly.

He sighed. "I didn't mean for it to come out like that."

Yep. That's what he said.

This is pointless." I took a step, but he grabbed my arm.

"I winced. My body was a minefield of bruises and Connor's hand was too large to avoid them.

"Sorry." He quickly released my arm. "Would you just listen? Please?"

I glared at him and leaned my head against the tree.

His feet shuffled and his posture straightened. "You've been judging me since the instant we met. Well, you know what? I'm sick of balancing on your scale. Would it kill you to give me a chance for once?"

His words stung, but the truth often did. I stopped myself from crossing my arms, not wanting to appear hostile. "Listening."

He took a step closer. "I screwed up. Big time. But I never betrayed you guys."

I snorted. "Really? 'Cause—"

His finger held my lips closed. "You said you were listening."

If I was really judging him, I'd use much stronger words than 'jerk'.

He kept his finger on my lips. "Look, I thought I could handle the situation."

I pushed his hand away. "Situation? You mean Gina? Because it looked like you were handling her just fine."

His jaw flung open.

"It's okay. I get it. I was ... what? Pre-season, preparing you for the real game?"

"No—"

"The hors d'oeuvre before the main course?"

"Lib—"

"But it's my fault." I continued. "Because I did give you a chance. I dared to think that you could be different than every other man in my life. I wanted to believe that I could ... have feelings for you and you would return them."

My eyes started watering as my anger and disappointment surfaced. "I should have listed to my gut, but none of that matters now. This isn't about *us*. There is no *us*. This is about what you did to Ashley."

"Shh." He put his hand on the tree above my head and leaned into it, invading my personal space. "Can I talk now?"

His face was inches from mine. Glorious heat radiated from his body, and I longed to be closer—warmer.

Talk?

He accepted my silence as permission to speak. "Alright, Your Honor, you are judging this case based primarily on circumstantial evidence."

I raised my eyebrow at him.

Has his voice always been this sensual?

"You allowed events that you witnessed to discredit the facts that you know." He tapped my head.

I nodded, convinced that talking probably wasn't the best idea.

He smiled. "Since evidence is non-existent, we must rely on facts. Fact one—," he held up a finger, "—no matter what you saw, or what you think you saw, I love Ashley."

My head swam from the steel-earth-musk scent of Connor. What had I seen? Had there been something that made me question his love for Ashley? I envisioned the night he told me she was his daughter, remembering the love in his eyes as he watched her sleep.

"I acted with only her best interests in mind. As her father and a Soldier, I did what I believed to be right."

My brain scrambled to find the relating puzzle pieces and snap them into place.

"Fact two—," Connor held up a second finger, "—Gina Thompson is a soul-stealing, life-leeching, black hole from whom there is no escape."

My laughter surprised even myself. Connor smiled at me as my hand flew up to cover my mouth.

"Fact three—," a British accent accompanied the third finger. All humor vanished from his face as he leaned closer and tucked a stray curl behind my ear. His touch sent shivers down my spine as we locked eyes.

Breathe.

"I love you Liberty Collins." He leaned closer to me—just inches away.

My heart stopped.

I focused on his mouth as he approached. My breath caught and I snapped my eyes shut. His lips pressed against mine, and his whiskers gently tickled my skin.

Stupid, stupid, stupid.

But stupid felt so good. My response was instinctive. My hands found their way to his muscular chest, as his warm arm wrapped around my waist, pulling me even closer. His curious tongue continued its exploration of my mouth.

We stood suspended; lost in the moment.

He pulled away from me, his gaze steady and intense, turning my knees to Jell-O. The corner of his mouth curved into a smile as he slid behind me, placing his back against the tree.

"Come here Lib." He grabbed my hand and spun me to face him.

Warm arms wrapped around me and pulled me into the heat. I rested my head on his shoulder and breathed in his delicious scent. Closing my eyes I simply existed in his embrace, pushing away trepidation about my foolishness.

But fire is so much fun to play with ...

Connor chuckled and pulled my chin up, forcing me to look at him. "You scared me. I thought I'd lost you."

Lost me? You never had me.

I let out a deep breath and looked away. Being in his arms felt so good, but I knew it was a lie.

Can't work. Won't last.

"What Lib?" He unwrapped his arms and looked down at me. "Don't you love me?"

"I can't ... I won't be just another notch in your head board. I'm not that girl, Connor, not even for you." I blew out a breath. A strong breeze rushed by, robbing me of the body heat I'd borrowed from him. "I have to be true to who I am, and the person *I am* doesn't mesh well with *Washington's most eligible bachelor.*"

He scowled. "That's not fair. I was given that brand a long time ago." He shook his head. "I'm not that person anymore."

I studied his features, longing to be back in his warm embrace. "That's just it. How can I love you, when I don't even know *who* you are?"

"I'm not asking what you know in here." He tapped my forehead. "I'm asking what you feel in here." His finger meandered down my hair and traced circles over my heart.

My breathing quickened as panic took control of my senses. I had no idea how to respond; hadn't allowed myself to even consider the possibility. I'd fought those feelings so hard, that even the idea of revealing them terrified me.

As I stared at Connor my inner child called out for a rescue. Deep inside, I wanted all the things that any woman wants: happiness, security, love. But I knew these feelings never lasted, and often came with a price tag I was unwilling to pay.

"You don't have to answer now." His shoulders drooped as he allowed his weariness to surface. "It's been a rough few days, and this is a lot for me to unload on you. Just promise me that you'll think about it—about me. About us."

Us?

I gulped and nodded.

He kissed my forehead and walked back toward the cave, leaving me alone with my thoughts.

My mind raced as my breathing slowed. 'That's just a brand,' he'd said. I sighed.

Brand. Why would he use that word?

"Brands fade, but they never *really* go away," I mumbled, taking a step toward the camp.

'And who are you to limit me?'

The *call* surprised me after its extended absence. Power filled my body and drove me to my knees, reminding me that my God was not one to be confined. Tears rolled down my face while my heart flooded with love, peace, and understanding.

'I am the Alpha and Omega. Do you not believe I can change the heart of one man?'

You really know how to make an entrance.

I looked up, wondering if anyone could see me—if anyone could feel what I felt.

Connor continued to walk away, and the light from the fire framed his body, creating an aura that was almost angelic. With his head held high and shoulders back, his presence was commanding.

'That is your future.'

"Connor?" I asked. "You have got to be kidding me. I don't even *like* Connor." But even as I spoke the words that denied my feelings, they intensified. My heart swelled as I stared at him.

Oh no.

'That is your future. You will work together to heal my children and restore peace to my land.'

"Me?" I stared up at the sky. "I realize that Your choices have been somewhat narrowed, but me? Surely You can find someone more qualified for the job. I work in marketing, remember?" My eyes roved over the camp, finally settling on Connor who had sat down and was talking to one of the Soldiers.

"Does it matter that this is *not* what *I* want?"

His laughter swept over me; refreshing and invigorating like aloe on a sunburn. I closed my eyes and let it fill me to the brim until my own laughter blended with His.

'My child, you have no idea what you want.'

Liberty's Journal

July 4:

On this Independence Day, I have much to celebrate. We're still alive, still free, and even more importantly, my hope has been renewed.

In this time of sorrow, I have been shown happiness. Amidst a world of hate, I have been taught to love. I have learned that nothing is impossible, and no one is beyond redemption.

Jeff has found a new life with the army. He's been given something to believe in, and people who believe in him.

Ashley is healing. Her strength and resilience amazes me. Every day I am blessed by her presence, and she is my sunshine in times of rain.

Connor's has changed. As I watch him evolve into the man and leader he's fated to be, I can't help but wonder about "us." He has given me time to consider the possibility, and I am trying. I'm just not ready yet.

My life has changed so much. There is no Canada to flee to. No escape from the mistakes we have made—the destruction we have wrought.

Our country withers as the Progression thrives. Every day it claims lives, takes "volunteers," and destroys the principles America was founded on.

They must be stopped.

As we head south on another mission, I pray for enough strength to be the instrument God requires to help save His people and bring freedom back to His land.

We are troubled on every side, yet not distressed; we are perplexed, but not in despair; persecuted, but not forsaken; cast down, but not destroyed.
2 Corinthians 4:8-9